"Who are you?" Lily asked.

"Nate Coates. I'm the forest ranger here. I just happened to be out checking for signs of flooding when I found you."

"Lucky for me."

He must have heard the unshed tears in her voice, or [saw them on her] face, bec[ause his] hand in [her] palm see[med] ...les spiraling ...

"You su[re] ...

Genuine ... eyes. Fo[r] ... away fro[m] ... dared co... single fr... troubles... try to us...

Someone...

His firm ... She pull... [sm]ile. "I'm just...

"But a g[ood] ... your bab...

Books by Leigh Bale

Love Inspired

The Healing Place
The Forever Family
The Road to Forgiveness
The Forest Ranger's Promise
The Forest Ranger's Husband
The Forest Ranger's Child

LEIGH BALE

is a multiple award-winning author of inspirational romance, including a prestigious Golden Heart. She is the daughter of a retired U.S. forest ranger, holds a B.A. in history with distinction and is a member of Phi Kappa Phi Honor Society. She loves working, writing, grandkids, spending time with family, weeding the garden with her dog Sophie and watching the little sagebrush lizards that live in her rock flower beds. She has two married children and lives in Nevada with her professor husband of thirty-one years. Visit her website at www.LeighBale.com.

The Forest Ranger's Child

Leigh Bale

Recycling programs
for this product may
not exist in your area.

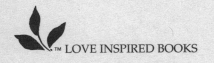 ™ LOVE INSPIRED BOOKS

ISBN-13: 978-0-373-87749-2

THE FOREST RANGER'S CHILD

Copyright © 2012 by Lora Lee Bale

www.LoveInspiredBooks.com

Printed in U.S.A.

For as in Adam all die,
even so in Christ shall all be made alive.
—*1 Corinthians* 15:22

This one is for Wade and Bonnie,
with whom I share something unique and
wonderful. Our childhood. I love you both dearly.
I always have and always will. No matter what.

And many thanks to Dan Baird,
consultant extraordinaire.

Chapter One

He wouldn't want her now. Not after what she'd done.

Lillian Hansen rested her left hand over her rounded stomach. Tears throbbed at the backs of her eyes. Her unborn child deserved a better mother than she could ever be. And yet, Lily couldn't help believing that out of all the mistakes she'd made in the past, fighting for this baby's life wasn't one of them.

She rolled down the windows of her red compact car. Taking a deep breath, she brushed a hand across the back of her damp neck, wishing the air conditioner worked. Drafts of hot, dusty air filtered through the vents as she drove through Jasper, Nevada, the small ranching town where she'd been raised.

The town hadn't changed much in the past seven years since she'd left home without saying goodbye. The two shabby grocery stores still faced each other across Main Street, Mallard's gas station stood at the end of the block with the one-room post office around the corner and the red brick church house near the city park. She knew them well.

The wheels of her car thumped over the railroad tracks as she headed outside of town. Within two miles, the asphalt gave way to gravel and then dirt road. With a quick twist of her wrist, she flipped off the radio. Nothing but scratchy static in this part of Nevada.

The April weather seemed unseasonably warm. Either that or her physical condition was making changes in her body she didn't understand. The warm breeze whipped at her long brown hair as she slowed her car and looked out at Emerald Valley. A hurtful pang of nostalgia caused her to suck back a breath. Memories swamped her as she gazed at the familiar view. Even though she'd turned her back on Dad and everything he'd tried to teach her, she still felt like she belonged here. She always had. She just hadn't known it back then.

She should have called the ranch first to make sure Dad was home. Getting into the house wouldn't be a problem. He never locked the front door. But it'd been three years since they'd spoken by phone. Three years since he'd begged her to come home and change her life. She'd hung up on him in anger. What would she do if he tossed her out the moment he saw her again? She had no other place to go. No job, no money, no friends and no husband.

Driving the road on autopilot, her gaze skimmed the fertile green fields filled with alfalfa and tall sedge grasses. Thin fingers of streams crisscrossed the valley, feeding off the numerous lakes higher up in the Ruby Mountains. Herds of black Angus cattle grazed lazily on the rich pasturelands. At the end of each creek bed, a ranch house and barn nestled at the base of the protective mountains.

Nothing much had changed. Except her.

The baby had been the catalyst that brought Lily to her senses. That and several blows from Tommy's fist. When she thought of all Tommy's empty promises, she could blame no one but herself. She'd stayed too long, making one poor choice after another. Clinging to the hope that he'd finally marry her. That he'd change and get control over his brutal temper.

And then came the final blow. He was already married.

It'd taken an unexpected pregnancy and a call from Tommy's wife to shock Lily into reality, and she promised never to look back. She had a child to think about now. A child to protect the way Dad had tried to protect her.

She shook her head, refusing to cry. Her tears had dried up long ago. Other than Dad, she wanted no other man in her life. Ever again.

Wow! Usually Jasper River was nothing more than a dry creek bed. Now, a stream of water ran through it. The winter must have been harsh, with deep snows still showing on the mountains. The unseasonably warm weather must be causing melt-off in the higher elevations.

Lily couldn't help being jarred from her thoughts as she turned the bend. The car backfired when she slowed it to a crawl. The narrow dirt road demanded attention as she neared the muddy streambed. Normally she should be able to drive right through on dry ground. She hoped her car wouldn't bottom out as she crossed. If she got a running start and gunned it, she should be able to rush her car right through and up to the opposite side of the road.

She pressed the accelerator and the motor revved. The car entered the riverbed at a good speed, but then the tires dragged, spinning in mud.

No, no! She couldn't get stuck here. Emerald Ranch was still a good five-mile walk and she didn't want to lug her suitcase all that way.

A dull roar filled her ears. What on earth—

Looking to her left, she widened her eyes. A rolling mound of sludge, clumps of sagebrush, rocks, tree limbs and debris filled the streambed. Headed straight toward her.

Lily gasped, terror flushing her heated skin.

Flash flood!

She floored the accelerator, gripping the steering wheel like a lifeline. "Come on! Get across!"

The tires spun in the mire. Panic climbed her throat. She'd heard stories about flash floods but had never seen one. Not like this.

The car wouldn't move. The tires whirred, making a shrill zipping sound.

Lily reached for the window controls, rolling up the glass pane on her side just as the muddy water slammed against the car. The force of the blow caved in the door and almost flipped the vehicle over on its side.

She screamed with fear and pain, crossing her arms over her round abdomen to protect her unborn child the only way she could. Her head jerked to the right like a raggedy doll. Thank goodness she still wore her seat belt, but no one would hear her cries. No one but her Heavenly Father.

The flood tossed the car around and Lily held on for dear life. Murky water poured through the open passenger window. The cold muck quickly soaked her clothes and she shivered. She turned her face away from the force of the icy water, gasping for breath.

A broken tree limb caught her eye. It whooshed past, carried by the swift current. She watched it in fascination, feeling broken and alone, just like that limb. How she wished the river could carry her heartache and guilt away as easily as it carried that tree branch.

For one fleeting moment, Lily considered letting the flood sweep her away. If she didn't fight it, she'd be carried downstream and buried beneath debris. Some rancher would find her days, perhaps weeks, later. She wouldn't have to face her shame anymore. No more worries or grinding fear. No baby. She wouldn't have to confront her father and his big, broken heart. A bit of pain and she could give up her life.

And then she'd have to face the Lord.

No! She shook her head, her knuckles whitening around the steering wheel. Something hardened inside of her. She wanted to live. Mom had told her God loved His children. All of them. It was never too late to seek forgiveness. Not if you really meant it and changed your life.

Her fingers clawed at the lever to free her seat belt, but it held firm. "Please, God, have mercy on us. I'll make things right. I'll become the woman You want me to be. I'll do what's right for this child. I promise."

Maybe it was too late for forgiveness. Maybe—

The car wheeled around, carried along by the swift strength of the current. The roar filled Lily's ears and she tried to steer the car, but it did no good. She found herself under control of the flood, just as she'd been under the control of evil forces. Finally, she'd found the strength to break free. To beg God's forgiveness and start anew.

Not this time. She couldn't break free of the flood. It held her in its grasp.

She sat waist-deep in muddy water. Several times, the force of the tide threatened to roll the car. She screamed again out of sheer terror. And then she forced herself to think. Think!

Should she climb out or stay put? Common sense told her she'd drown if she stayed inside. But if she got out of the car, she might not make it to shore. She was five and a half months pregnant. The powerful current might carry her along, beating her to death with churning rocks, trees and rubble.

What should she do?

"Please, God, give me one more chance."

As she let go of the steering wheel, a feeling of peace enveloped her. She pressed on the lever one more time hard, and her seat belt released its hold across her body. Crouching beside the open passenger window, she pressed her hands protectively over her stomach. Waves of love washed over her as she thought of the precious life she shielded. She owed everything to this child, who had set Lily back on the road toward the Lord.

Lily watched for the best opportunity, looking for a safe place to go. She'd have to swim hard and strong to make it to shore. To fight the churning tide.

Taking a deep breath, she pushed through the open window and felt the strong, cold current sweep her away. She was in God's hands now.

"You don't see something like this every day." Nathan Coates spoke to himself before whistling low beneath his breath. Sitting in his green Forest Service truck, he stared out the windshield at the flash flood, amazed by the melee of swirling, muddy water. It rolled past, expanding across the banks of the creek bed, slamming through everything in its path.

Opening the truck door, he picked up his camera and stepped outside. As he walked closer to the banks, he snapped pictures, wondering if the photos could do justice to the powerful, roaring waters. It must be raining hard up in the mountains. He'd never seen anything like this and stood in awe at Mother Nature's wrath.

Another sound made him pause and he turned his head downstream. Two tires and headlights peeked out above the curve of the riverbank, the rest of the red vehicle buried beneath a layer of mud and tattered bushes. He snapped a few pictures, then took several more steps and paused. Did he hear...

The sound came again. A scream for help!

Nate ran toward the grass edging the creek. His booted feet sank in mud as he hurried through tall sedges and willows.

The growl of the flood swallowed the sound and he doubted his senses. He paused at the edge of the swollen river, paying attention in case a second wave of water exceeded the banks and pulled him into the flood. He scanned the melee, thinking he'd imagined the cry.

There! A woman, buried to her chin in water as she clung to a boulder in the middle of the stream. Her long brown hair lay plastered to her pale face, her eyes closed as she cried hoarsely. "Help me. Please!"

"I see you!" He waved.

She opened her eyes, but fear or fatigue kept her from moving. If she let go, the flood would sweep her away.

He cupped one hand around his mouth like a megaphone and yelled louder. "Hang on! I'll be right back."

She didn't even lift a hand as he turned and sprinted to his truck. Mentally, he took stock of the supplies he had in the back tool chest. His fire pack, ready at a moment's notice in case he was called out on a wildfire. It included fresh water and food. A first-aid kit, which he might need soon. A toolbox, coils of rope and rappelling clips. He'd definitely need those now.

A sense of urgency pushed him to hurry. He had no idea how long she'd be able to hold on.

Inside his truck, he tossed the camera onto the seat and started the engine. Putting the vehicle into four-wheel drive, he steered it off the dirt road and through the brush, getting as close to the flood as possible without burying the tires in the bog so that he wouldn't be able to break free.

She was still there, her right cheek resting against the hard boulder. Water rushed over her, slapping her in the face. Now and then she coughed and he breathed with relief. Obviously she had a good hold on the rock, but how long would her strength hold out against the cold, swift current?

After jerking on a pair of leather gloves, Nate secured two lengths of rope to the front fender of the truck. Then he tied one rope around his middle. As an Eagle Scout, he'd learned to tie knots that wouldn't come loose, thanks to his mother's persistence to keep him involved in good activities.

Binding the other rope to his belt, he trudged through the

mud toward the flood. He gasped as he entered the frigid water. The powerful stream knocked him down, soaking his green forest ranger uniform to the skin. The rope gave him security and he pulled it taut to regain his feet. Without the lifeline, he would have been swept away by the stream and possibly drowned.

With powerful strokes, he fought to swim his way across to the woman. Adrenaline pumped through his body, giving him strength. An entire tree trunk brushed past, its sharp branches scraping his side. In the freezing water, he grunted but barely felt the pain.

Thankfully the majority of rocks and debris had already passed, pushed forward by the flood. Every muscle in Nate's body tensed as he fought to keep from being whisked away. He barely dodged a boulder aimed at his head. Cold water washed over him again and again and he coughed.

Almost there.

His cold fingers clasped the rock the woman was clinging to, his wet gloves stiff and unyielding. Panting for breath, he looped the rope around the boulder to hold him steady until he was ready to return to shore. He leaned next to the woman, speaking loud over the roar of water. "You okay?"

Her eyes slit open, then closed, followed by a subtle nod. She was alive, but a trail of blood rolled down her forehead where a lump had formed beneath a nasty gash. Without examining her, he had no idea of the seriousness of her injuries.

"Help us. Please," she whispered in a hoarse voice.

"Us? Is someone with you?" He looked around, his gaze searching for another person he must have missed, but he saw no one else.

She didn't respond, her eyes rolling backward in her head. She let go of the rock and he grabbed her before she could whisk away. Holding her tightly by the arm, he pulled the second rope free of his belt and tied it around her chest, just beneath her arms.

"Can you hear me?" He patted her chilled cheeks, hoping to rouse her. He'd need her help to get them both safely back to shore.

She didn't open her eyes, but her mouth moved. He leaned near, feeling her warm breath against his cheek.

"My baby…please don't let my baby die…sorry for everything…so sorry."

She was pregnant!

If Nate hadn't felt the critical situation before, he did now. He had to get her out of here and rush her to a doctor.

"I'm gonna pull us back to shore, okay?"

She gave a brief nod, her eyes opening. In their velvet brown depths, he saw deep, wrenching fear.

"Can you hold on to me?" he asked.

Another nod that didn't inspire much confidence in him. She seemed too weak. Too fragile and exhausted. But he doubted he could save her if she couldn't help hold on.

"Wrap your arms and legs around me like a python and don't let go no matter what. I'll pull us to safety."

She did as told, lying against his back as she knotted her small hands in a fist across his chest. With her behind him, he took hold of the rope and pulled, hand-over-hand. The current swept them away and the woman cried out but she didn't let go.

"I've got us. Just hang on." His words were meant to encourage her and to give himself the nerve to keep going.

The rope burned through his hands, but he found a harder grip. Thank goodness for his gloves. His palms would have been shredded to the bone without the protective layer.

He and the woman jerked hard, tossed in the water like a tiny twig. He pulled and pulled until his arms trembled with fatigue. The frigid water sapped his strength. If he let go, they'd lose headway and he'd have to start over. They still could drown. His stamina wouldn't last forever. He must make every movement count.

He didn't look up, focusing on the length of rope directly in front of him. It was a gargantuan effort not to let his gloved hands slip again. His fingers felt like clumps of ice and wouldn't obey his commands. Hand-over-hand. Again and again. How long was this rope?

Finally! Finally he felt solid ground beneath his feet. He kept walking, carrying the woman on his back as he trudged up the muddy bank, his booted feet sinking deep. He staggered to shore.

Rivulets of water drained from his drab olive-green shirt and pants. As he walked, his work boots felt like heavy bricks of cement strapped to his feet. Looking down, he noticed he'd lost his ranger shield, a small hole in his shirt showing the only proof that he'd worn the badge that day. Blood soaked his side where the tree branch had lacerated his shirt and skin. He scanned the injury with his eyes. Just a flesh wound. He'd survived worse injuries riding wild broncs on the national rodeo circuit, but he'd never been this scared even when he'd faced an angry bull.

He dropped his hands to the shore and the woman slid away. She lay on the ground beside him, her blue jeans splotched with dirt. One foot was bare, her tennis shoe and sock obviously sucked away by the flood. Her wet shirt clung to her rounded tummy. Definitely pregnant but not real big yet.

He knelt beside her, touching her face with his shaking hands, searching for life. "You okay, ma'am?"

A single, brief nod.

"How about your baby?"

In response, she slid a pale hand over her abdomen. He had no idea if her baby was alive. He'd heard of traumatic events like this throwing a woman into early labor. She didn't look far enough along for the baby to survive if it were born now.

A sense of urgency swept him. "Can you stand?"

This time, she didn't move or open her eyes.

Standing, he tried to pick her up and almost dropped her in spite of her slim weight. The effort to get her to shore had sapped the strength in his arms.

Changing his tactics, he untied the ropes from around them, then took hold of her shoulders and half carried, half dragged her to his truck. Once he got her inside and buckled in, he wrapped a woolen blanket over her, tucking it around her shoulders and feet. The chattering of her teeth told him she was still alive and suffering from the beginnings of hypothermia. The shivering would help warm her body, but he had no idea what the impact might be on her baby.

With slow, awkward movements, he removed the roped clips from the fender and tossed them aside in the brush. He climbed inside and started the engine before turning on the heater full-bore. He had to get her warm. He breathed deeply, wanting to rest but not daring to do so yet.

With jerky movements, he shifted the truck into gear and turned it around in the sagebrush. As he headed back to town, he sped all the way. The truck bounced over the rutted road like a flat basketball hitting pavement.

Glancing at the woman, he noticed her chest moved with each shallow breath she took. She murmured several words, not making any sense. Her spiked eyelashes lay closed against smooth, ashen skin. Her long hair lay in sodden, dark strands around her shoulders. Even in this condition, he could tell she was beautiful. With her thin arms and legs, he couldn't help wondering how she'd clung to that rock. How long had she been out there? He hoped she hadn't suffered any trauma to her abdomen. How had she survived the ordeal?

Within fifteen minutes, he pulled into the parking lot of the small clinic in town. He pressed on the horn long and hard to draw attention, then stumbled around the truck to open the door and get the woman out. His strength had recovered a bit and he picked her up, staggering to the sidewalk where Clara Richens met him with a wheelchair.

"What happened?" the nurse asked.

He set the unconscious woman in the chair. Her head rolled back, her hands resting lifelessly in her lap. She looked dead and a blaze of panic overwhelmed Nate. She just couldn't die. Not on his watch.

"She was caught in a flash flood in Emerald Valley." Together, he helped Clara wheel the woman inside.

"Do you know who she is?" Clara eyed his soggy clothes and bloodstained shirt.

"No. I just found her and pulled her from the flood." He stood back on wobbly legs.

Clara looked at the woman's face, her eyes filled with sympathy. And then her expression changed to stunned recognition. "Oh, my goodness. It's Lily!"

"What? You know her?" Nate asked.

Without another word, Clara motioned to an orderly to come and help.

As they whisked the woman away, Nate called after them. "She's pregnant and worried about her baby."

Clara nodded. "I can see that. I'll warn the doctor."

They disappeared behind the swinging double doors and Nate just stood there, adrenaline and fear pumping through his body. Clara must know the woman.

Lily. A pretty flower, just like the woman he'd rescued.

"Nate, you look awful. What happened?"

Nathan turned to find Shelby Larson standing beside him. In this small town, almost everyone knew everyone else by name. Shelby was married to Matt, Nate's ranger assistant.

A pleasantly plump woman, she wore a white nurse's smock on top of her street clothes.

"Hi, Shelby. It's been quite a day." He chuckled and raked a hand through his damp hair before explaining the events that had led him to the clinic.

She touched his arm. "Come with me so I can take a look at that wound on your side. Maybe we've got some dry clothes around here somewhere."

"It's okay. I've got an extra change of clothes in my fire pack. I'll get them and be right back."

"But your wound…"

"It's just a scratch. I'll let you look at it in just a moment."

He left, going to retrieve the spruce-green Nomex pants and yellow fire-resistant shirt from his fire pack before returning and changing in the privacy of an examination room. He had two extra pairs of dry socks and pulled one pair on before shoving his feet back into his damp cowboy boots. If he didn't wear the boots until they dried, they'd be ruined.

Shelby cleaned the deep scratches on his side and bandaged them. No big deal. They'd heal up fine.

Back outside in the reception room, Nate slumped on the sofa and borrowed Shelby's cell phone to call his office at the ranger's station. His cell phone had been ruined by water and his people should know what had happened and where he was.

"You don't know who the woman is?" Margaret, his office manager, asked.

"Nope, but Clara Richens recognized her. Her car's still out there, buried in the riverbed. She probably got caught in the flood when she tried to cross the stream. Can you make some phone calls to each of the ranchers in Emerald Valley? Warn them to use the Bailey bridges or stay put. I don't want anyone else trying to cross a flooding stream until it stops raining up in the mountains."

"Will do."

"And Margaret? Ask Matt if he'd mind driving out and checking the status of the flood. Tell him not to cross it or do anything that might get him hurt, but see if the flood has passed yet."

"You got it. You take care and check in with us later, okay?"

Nate hung up the cell phone, his body feeling wilted, his mind full of activity. What if the woman lost her baby? What if she died after all? Somehow he felt responsible for her. His heart went out to her and her child. He should call her husband, but had no idea who that might be. Her ID was probably still in her car.

He stood and approached the front counter. "Any news yet?"

Shelby shook her head. "I'm sorry. The doctor's still with her."

An hour later, Nate had laid his head back against the sofa in the waiting room to rest. Dr. Kenner came down the hall, a stethoscope dangling around his thick neck. Nate breathed a sigh of relief and stood. Finally some news.

"Hi, Nate." The doctor smiled, his bald head and ruddy cheeks flushed with color.

"How is she?"

"She'll be fine. She's resting now. A very lucky young woman. What you did was heroic."

Nate ignored that remark. He didn't feel heroic. He just felt worried. "And her baby?"

"The baby seems fine. Strong heartbeat, vigorous movement. Lily's almost six months along, but she didn't receive any trauma to her abdomen, just her head. She took eight stitches in her scalp, but that'll heal soon enough."

"Lily is her name?" The delicate flower of the resurrection.

"Yeah, Lily Hansen. Hank Hansen's girl. I was there when her momma died after being bucked off one of those wild mustangs she loved to ride. She trained horses for the rodeo. Quite rare for a woman."

She sounded like Nate's kind of gal.

"I didn't know Hank had any kids."

"Just Lily."

A twinge of sympathy pinched Nate's heart. Hank owned Emerald Ranch and was one of the grazing permittees on the national forest. Hank kept to himself for the most part, but he and Nate had become friends. Both men had ridden the national rodeo circuit at one time. Even so, Hank was one of the most irascible men Nate had ever met. If he'd lost his wife in a horse-related accident, Nate could understand why. The man also seemed to be having some financial troubles of late. "Last I heard, Hank was ailing. Heart attack or something."

The doctor didn't respond and Nate figured the man knew the details but was maintaining patient confidentiality.

"It's probably good that his daughter has come home to take care of him," Nate said.

"Yeah, she grew up here in Jasper, but she left right after high school. After her mom died, she and her dad didn't get along too well. I've just called Hank to let him know she's here. He's driving into town as soon as he can."

Nate frowned, hoping the rancher didn't try to pass the stream while it was still flooding. Hank should use the high Bailey bridge the Army Corp of Engineers had constructed across the river a couple of weeks ago.

They chatted for several more minutes, mostly with Nate asking questions the doctor did his best not to answer.

"She's waking up. You can go in and see her for a few minutes if you like."

"Me?" Nate hesitated.

Dr. Kenner clapped a hand on Nate's back and smiled broadly. "You're the man who saved her. Shelby will take you back."

Shelby stepped around the front counter to guide Nate down the hallway. A happy smile beamed on her face. "What a great day. Lily took up with a n'er-do-well from Reno and broke her daddy's heart. He'll be so happy to see her again. This story is sure to make the evening news. You're a hero, Nate. You saved her life."

As Nate's heels thudded against the tiled floor, he didn't feel like a hero. He felt like a worried husband and father, which wasn't right. This wasn't his wife and child. He knew nothing about Lily Hansen or her life, yet he couldn't stop worrying about her. Her pitiful cries for help still tore at his heart. They each could have died today and he realized how precious life was.

For some odd reason, Nate hesitated at the door to Lily's room, looking in at her still form lying on the narrow hospital bed. Wrapped in sterile blankets, she looked so helpless. So cold and vulnerable.

He'd saved this woman and her unborn child. He couldn't help remembering what his mom had taught him about being his brother's keeper. Some cultures believed if you saved someone's life, you were then responsible for them until the day you died. A heavy thought indeed. Being responsible for Lily Hansen and her baby the rest of his life made his insides jittery.

Protecting Lily Hansen was her husband's job.

As he stepped into the room, Nate felt as though he were walking off the precipice of a cliff, prepared to hit the jagged rocks below. And somehow he knew his life had just irrevocably changed. He'd never be the same again.

Chapter Two

Lily slowly opened her eyes, moving her head on a lumpy pillow. Thin blankets covered her and someone had dressed her in a hospital gown. From the dim spray of sunlight streaming through the window, she could tell it was late afternoon.

Her head hurt and she lifted a hand, finding a small bandage covering the right side of her forehead. She flinched as the memory of the flood rushed into her mind. And her rescue.

Scanning the small hospital room, she swiveled toward the door…and froze. *He* stood there. The man who had saved her life.

Correction: *their* lives. Hers and her baby girl's.

She pressed a hand to her abdomen and breathed with relief when the baby wiggled against her palm. Thank the Lord her child was okay.

The man had his hands slung low in his pants pockets. A long-sleeved, yellow shirt covered his powerfully built arms and shoulders. His dark, damp hair had been slicked back, freshly combed. Green pants clung to his long, muscled legs. He looked ready to fight a forest fire.

Who was he?

"Hi, there." He spoke softly, his deep voice sending a shiver over her body.

"You…you saved our lives." In spite of her ordeal, she remembered every bit of what had happened with perfect clarity. The terror and pain in her head. The bursting hope when this man had tied a lifeline around her and dragged her to shore. The way he'd pulled her to his truck when she was too weak to move. And then tucked a coarse blanket around her before driving like a madman into town. After that, she couldn't remember anything. At first, she thought it had been a nightmare, that she'd just imagined it all. Now she knew it was real.

He removed his hands from his pockets and stepped toward her. Her gaze lowered to his belt buckle. She immediately recognized it. Decorated with silver belt plate and gold overlay, it showed a cowboy astride a bucking horse. A national rodeo circuit all-around cowboy belt buckle. Tommy had always wanted one but wasn't good enough to earn it.

Her rescuer was a rodeo man, just like Tommy. In an instant, she wanted nothing more to do with Nate.

She tensed, her throat convulsing as she swallowed. She'd prayed for help and the Lord had performed a miracle for her. And now that miracle stood in front of her. A tall, strong man with a lean, athletic body.

In one glance, Lily sized him up. His determined, graceful movements, a firm mouth, stubborn chin and piercing brown eyes. She'd seen his kind before. Always in control. Forceful and unyielding.

The kind of man she wanted to avoid at all costs.

"How are you feeling?" He stood beside her bed, too close for comfort.

She stared up at him, trying to form the words to thank him. But her tongue felt like a leaden weight inside her mouth. Her gaze locked with his and her face burned with embarrassment. And then a wave of recognition hit her. As if she knew this man from somewhere but she couldn't quite place him. A feeling of trust and safety washed over her. Like she'd been reunited with her best friend after a long absence.

Calm as a summer's morning.

What an odd notion! She shook her head, thinking she must have hit her head very hard indeed to be thinking such things. She would never trust another man as long as she lived. The price was too high.

She blinked and looked away. "I'm fine. Thanks to you. I owe you a lot."

Okay, she didn't want to lay her gratitude on too thick, but she did feel thankful, didn't she?

Yes! In spite of everything, she wanted to make things right again. Mom had told her she could do anything with the Lord's help. And that's what she planned to do.

"You don't owe me anything. I did what anyone would have done." His voice sounded low and husky.

Again her gaze lifted to his. Again, a sweet feeling of contentment rested over her. A sentiment she hadn't felt in a long, long time. She decided to ignore it. "But it wasn't just anyone. It was you. And I'm appreciative. More than I can say."

"It was my pleasure. I'm just glad you're both okay." His gaze flickered briefly to her stomach and he smiled.

The expression crinkled his brown eyes at the corners and deepened a dimple in his right cheek. So familiar. So comfortable. Yet she knew she'd never met this man before today. So why did she feel like she knew him?

He knew about her baby. And she was too far along to pretend. Anyone could see that she was expecting. But she didn't want to discuss her disgrace with him. No doubt the news would be all over town by supper. The nurse and orderly had been in her room when the doctor visited her. The technician who had taken her blood. They all knew. In this small community, word spread fast. The prodigal daughter had returned. Pregnant with no husband.

A tremor of shame swept her and she inhaled an unsteady breath.

He jerked a thumb toward the door. "The doctor's contacted your father."

She almost groaned out loud. She'd wanted her reunion with Dad to be in private, out at the ranch. Not here in the hospital where so many people might overhear their conversation. Hopefully Dad wouldn't cause a scene. She had no idea if the doctor had told him about the baby, or if that would be her job. Either way, Dad would have to be told that she wasn't married.

"Who are you?" she asked.

"Nathan Coates. Most people just call me Nate. I'm the forest ranger here in Jasper. I just happened to be out checking for signs of flooding when I found you."

"Lucky for me." She spoke the words half-heartedly, still unable to dredge up much joy over her situation.

He must have heard the unshed tears in her voice, or seen some forlorn emotion on her face because he reached out and took her hand in his. The warmth of his calloused palm seeped through her skin and sent tingles spiraling up her arm.

"You sure you're okay?"

Genuine concern gleamed in his expressive eyes. For several moments, she couldn't look away from his handsome face, wishing she dared confide in him. Wishing she had one single friend in this world she could tell her troubles to that wouldn't hurt or betray her, or try to use her in some way.

Someone who would never lie to her.

His firm, lean fingers tightened around hers, no wedding ring on his left hand. Tommy hadn't worn a ring either, but he'd lied so many times. She'd been such a fool.

She pulled away from Nate and forced a smile. "I'm just tired. It's been a difficult day."

"That it has. But you're safe now, and your baby's gonna be fine."

He knew about her father, which meant the doctor or staff had blabbed her identity. So much for her quiet return home. But the friendly way Nate spoke to her brought another whoosh of familiarity. Why did she like this man in spite of her desire not to?

"Did they say when I can go home?" She glanced at the door, trying to ignore his engaging grin.

"I overheard the doctor telling the nurse you can leave the day after tomorrow. He wants to make sure your baby is okay first. But I should let him talk to you about that."

"Yes." She definitely didn't want to discuss her unborn child with this enigmatic man.

"I know your father well. He's a good man," he said.

"Yes, he is." And she realized she meant it. Somehow, being away from home so long had given her a lot of insight into what really mattered. Even though she'd thought she hated Dad when she left, she now realized she loved him very much. He'd been a good father in his own gruff way. Never once had he raised a hand to her. But he'd never told her he loved her, either. But he and Mom had taught her all about horses, something they each dearly loved. And he'd taught her about the Lord, although she'd ignored it at the time.

"Have you been away from home long?" Nate asked.

Yep, just as predicted. Here came the battery of questions. Next would come the fake smiles and soft gestures that soon turned rough when she wouldn't do what he wanted. Over her dead body would she allow a man to use force against her again.

"For a while." She didn't want to get close to this or any man.

"Where have you—"

"Ahem! Lily?"

Someone cleared their throat behind Nate and he turned as Lily looked past him at the door. "Daddy!"

Hank Hansen stepped forward, dressed in faded blue jeans and scuffed cowboy boots. He looked leaner than she remembered, with barely a rounded stomach hanging over his belt buckle. He held his shabby cowboy hat in his hands, his gray eyes narrowed with concern.

Nate stepped away and smiled respectfully as Hank came to stand beside Lily's bed. She'd promised herself she wouldn't cry when she saw her father again, but the baby and nearly losing her life today blew that vow right out the window. Tears burned her eyes, but she wouldn't let them fall.

As she looked at her father's weathered face, she felt surprised by the silver streaks in his hair and more wrinkles around his eyes and mouth. A burst of joy coiled through her chest. How glad she was to see him again. To be home, if only until her child was born.

"Daddy," she whispered, not knowing what else to say.

His chin quivered, his mouth tight. "Lily, I didn't believe it when they called to say you were here. But my little darlin' has really come home."

Dad leaned over and hugged her, squashing his hat between them. The brush of his whiskers scratched her cheek. She breathed him in, the scent of horses and peppermint. Never wanting to let go. Maybe he'd changed in the past seven years. Maybe he'd softened just a bit.

He held her several moments, something he'd done only once before, the day her mother died. Finally. Finally a show of loving emotion from him. How she needed this hug and she clung to him tightly.

Finally he pulled away and she brushed at her eyes. Dad coughed, a wrenching sound deep down in his lungs. He must be more overcome by emotion than she first thought.

Dad glanced at the forest ranger before clasping Nate's hand and pounding him hard on the back. "Thank you, Nate. Thank you so much. I'm grateful you were there to save my little girl."

Nate's face flushed with awkwardness, as if he didn't know quite how to react. "You're welcome, Hank. I'm glad to have helped."

Dad stood smiling between them and the silence ticked by. Lily couldn't help wondering how much Dad knew about her circumstance. Did he know about the baby? That she'd disgraced herself and their family name?

"Well, I better get going. It was a pleasure to meet you, Miss Hansen." Nate nodded respectfully to her, then took a step.

"Thanks again," Dad called.

"Yes, thank you," she agreed.

Nate waved and smiled before closing the door. And with his departure, Lily felt even more alone.

Nate couldn't explain the elation filling his chest. This day could have ended in tragedy, but it hadn't. He'd remember these events as long as he lived. And yet, he sensed something wrong here. Something he couldn't put his finger on.

As he stood at the receptionist's desk in the small clinic and waited for Shelby to get off the phone, troubling thoughts tugged at his brain. Obviously Hank Hansen was happy to see his daughter, but she seemed so reserved. Frightened even. Her short, almost curt answers when Nate had tried to find out about her. Her tensed posture and wary glances at the door, as if she longed to escape. And then, when Nate had turned to leave her alone with her father, an expression of pure panic had filled her eyes. As if she didn't want him to go.

Boy, was Nate getting mixed signals from her. He leaned his forearms against the high counter, fighting the confusion in his mind. The doctor had said Lily and her dad hadn't gotten along after her mother's death. Even with their happy reunion, it appeared that she and her father had a lot of past history that needed to be sorted out. Nate had no right to worry about the woman he'd saved, but he did all the same.

"I can't believe you did this. What would your mother say? I'm disappointed in you, Lily. More than I can say."

Nate turned, startled to hear the angry words coming from Lily's room. Hank's voice boomed behind the closed door, rushing up the empty hallway.

The door burst open and Hank came stomping out, his hat gripped in his fist, his face red as a charging bull. As the man stormed past, he coughed hard and didn't even glance at Nate. Shelby looked up from her desk, the phone still pressed against her ear, her mouth dropping open in surprise.

Nate stared after Hank as the man trudged through the automatic glass doors and out to the parking lot. Nate felt as though a tornado had just blown through the room. What had happened?

A muffled sob came from Lily's room and Nate swiveled around and walked to her door. Peering inside, he found her lying on her side facing the wall, her arms wrapped over her baby bump. Even though she made no sound, her thin shoulders trembled. She was obviously crying and his chest tightened with regret. How he hated to see a woman cry.

He rapped his knuckles against the door, wondering what he should say. Wondering how saving her life had made him feel so protective of her.

She glanced over her shoulder and looked startled and self-conscious. She rubbed her reddened eyes with the backs of her hands and sat up quickly, her nose dripping. When she rested her small hands protectively over her tummy, he couldn't help staring. How fragile she looked.

"What do you want?" Her voice sounded like a croak.

He reached for a tissue on the bedside stand and handed it to her. She whisked it from his fingers and blew her nose.

"I don't mean to intrude, but I couldn't help overhearing. I was wondering if I can do anything for you," he said.

"No, nothing. I'm fine." Her voice cracked and so did his heart.

"Are you hungry?"

She laughed and shook her head. "All you men are alike. You just don't get it, do you?"

"Get what?"

The velvety softness of her brown eyes pinned him with fury. "I don't want anything from you. Not now. Not ever."

Okay…

"I didn't mean to intrude, ma'am. I'll leave you alone." He turned to go, but she called him back.

"Wait!" Her features softened with regret. "Look, I…I don't mean to be ungrateful. It's just that I don't want to become involved again."

She bit her bottom lip and closed her eyes, her hands clenched. He stood there dumbfounded.

"Why can't this ever get easier?" She opened her eyes and looked at him.

"I'm sorry, but I don't understand." Nate wondered what he'd walked into. He had no idea if this woman was mentally unstable or just overwrought from her ordeal. He'd heard pregnant women had lots of hormones running through their bodies that caused a roller coaster of emotions. And Lily had been through a traumatic event today. He decided keeping his silence might be the best thing for him to do.

"I'm pregnant," she said.

He nodded, trying to comprehend. Wishing right now that he were anywhere but here. "Yes, I know."

"And I've never been married," she blurted.

He released a giant huff of air, finally understanding. Joyful and saddened by this news all at the same time. "And your father isn't happy about that?"

"No. Neither am I, but there's nothing I can do about it now. I...I wanted to be married." Her voice sounded small. "My father hates me."

"Ah, I'm sure he doesn't hate you."

"Yes, he does."

She stared at her stomach and a strand of russet hair swept past her face. Nate's fingers itched to tuck it back behind her ear, but he resisted the urge. He didn't know how to comfort her. He'd been raised by a single mother in a small, traditional town, and knew how hard it could be. Lily must be frightened half to death.

"Hank doesn't hate you. He's just hurting right now, but he'll get over it. He was sure happy to see you. He'll remember that once the shock of your pregnancy wears off." Nate didn't know why he was comforting her. When he'd been old enough to understand, his mother had explained that she'd conceived him out of wedlock and become the pariah of the town. Nate's father had deserted her. Her father disowned her. She'd had no friends and no support. To earn a living, she'd worked as a waitress until she'd died shortly after Nate graduated from high school. The hard life had taken its toll, breaking her body and spirit. Now, Nate hated the thought of Lily Hansen and her innocent child going through the same thing simply because she'd made a mistake.

"I don't know if he'll come back to get me or not." A plump tear rolled down her cheek and she dashed it away.

"Don't worry, he'll be here."

"How do you know?" She frowned at him. "I don't even know why I'm telling you all of this. I'm really thankful for what you did today, but please leave now, before I make a bigger spectacle of myself than I already have."

There was no anger in her words, just resignation. Someone had done a pretty good job of alienating this woman to make her so distrustful. Nate was smart enough to realize she wasn't herself right now, but her words wounded him just the same.

He nodded, wondering why he'd allowed himself to get sucked into her troubles with her father. She was right. He didn't belong here. "I'm sorry to have disturbed you."

Turning on his heel, he headed for the door, brushing past Shelby as she came in carrying a pitcher of water.

"You okay, honey?" Shelby asked.

"I'll be fine," came Lily's throaty reply.

Nate left the clinic, planning to return to work. Planning to forget the exchange he'd overheard between Hank and his daughter. Or that he'd ever saved the life of a beautiful woman named Lily Hansen.

Chapter Three

Two days later, Nate gripped the steering wheel of his truck and wondered what he was doing here at the clinic parking lot so early in the morning. He'd called the clinic each day to check up on Lily Hansen and find out when the doctor would release her. So much for forgetting their discussion when she'd asked him to leave.

He must be crazy, but he couldn't get her off his mind. Couldn't forget her desperate situation or the fact that she was about to become a mother.

After pacing the floor of his Forest Service house most of the night, he'd decided worrying about the small woman he'd rescued had become a full-time job. What would become of her if her father didn't return and take her home? That question alone had pushed Nate to drive to the clinic instead of in to work.

He'd been sitting here for almost two hours, watching and waiting. He didn't have a clue what he'd do if Hank didn't come for her.

Rolling down the window, Nate inhaled a deep breath of fresh, spring air. Morning sunshine glinted off the hood of his truck and he lifted an arm to shield his eyes. Yellow daffodils filled the flower bed edging the sidewalk. What a beautiful day. Now if Hank would show up, Nate could clear his conscience and be on his way to the office.

A rusty green pickup truck pulled into the parking lot. Nate leaned forward and squinted his eyes. Was that Hank Hansen?

Yes! The truck stopped in front of the automatic double doors of the clinic.

Nate sat back and released a satisfied sigh. Hank had come for his daughter, which meant everything was okay. Otherwise, the doctor wouldn't let Lily go home today. And for some reason, that pleased Nate enormously.

As predicted, the older man went inside, carrying a small brown bag. Within twenty-five minutes, he reappeared with Shelby pushing Lily in a wheelchair. Lily's delicate hands were folded over her stomach. Glimmers of sunshine glinted off her long russet hair, showing highlighted streaks of auburn. Even from this distance, Nate remembered the velvet softness of her brown eyes. The smattering of freckles sprinkled across her pert nose. He sure wished he could see her smile just once.

With her feet propped up on the footrest of the chair, she wore a red sweater, a pair of blue jeans and tennis shoes. Hank must have brought the clothing to her. Nate had no idea where Hank had gotten the clothes because Lily had just returned home and all her possessions were still buried in her mud-coated car. At least Hank was taking care of her.

They didn't notice him as Shelby helped Lily stand. Hank didn't smile as he opened the door and stood back while Lily climbed inside the old truck. She brushed past her father, staring straight ahead, her spine stiff.

Hostile.

Shelby closed the door and waved goodbye. And then Hank got into the truck and drove away. Not one word passed between them.

Nate wished he dared speak to Lily. At least she had a

place to stay, but her relationship with her father didn't look like it'd improved much. The thought of Hank upsetting Lily in her condition bothered Nate. No matter what was going on between them, Lily's unborn child needed protection.

So did she.

Starting the ignition, Nate put his vehicle into gear and pressed the accelerator. He tried to tell himself to think about the timber study sitting on his desk at work. Tried not to care.

Maybe he should pay a visit to Emerald Ranch later on. Then again, maybe he should mind his own business and stay far away from Lily Hansen and her father.

The sound of the rumbling engine filled Lily's ears as she sat tense in her seat. The silence between her and Dad grew louder by the minute.

She'd clicked on her seat belt before loosening the strap across the swell of her lower abdomen. A blanket of contentment rested over her. Her baby was okay. The little girl's heartbeat was strong and Lily had felt several hard thumps earlier that morning, the stirrings of life inside of her.

"You hungry?" Dad asked without looking at her.

"No, thank you."

They drove down Main Street and headed outside of town with several more minutes passing in silence.

"You're lucky Nate Coates found you when he did. He's a good man. He rode the professional rodeo circuit before he got injured like me. He won all-around cowboy fifteen years ago. Then he went to college to become a forest ranger."

Lily bit her tongue to keep from uttering a derogative statement. Tommy had traveled often so he could compete in rodeos. She'd waited at home for his return, wondering why he never seemed to win anything. And then his wife had called. Tommy had been cheating on both of them with one-night stands in every town. Buckle babes who followed the rodeo circuit looking for nothing but a good time. When Lily had confronted Tommy with the truth, he'd...

No! She wouldn't think about that now. Never again would Lily subject herself to that kind of treatment. Maybe she deserved it, but her child didn't.

In her younger years, Dad had been gone all the time, competing on the professional circuit. Until a bull had gored his shoulder and ended his career. Lily had no desire to be friends with a rodeo-going forest ranger. No sirree.

"I suppose you'll need some new clothes," Dad said. "Your bedroom's just as you left it, but I doubt there're many clothes in the closet that'll fit you now."

"I'll make out fine with what's there, Dad." Even if she had to wash the clothes on her back every night, she would not ask her father for another single thing other than food. She remembered she had some oversize T-shirts in one of her dresser drawers and would wear them.

He cleared his throat. "We'll drive into Reno for some shopping. Maybe on Friday, after you've had a couple of days to rest."

"I don't want to put you out."

"You've got to have clothes." His stubborn tone sounded final.

She angled her body to face him and reached out to briefly touch his arm. "I'm sorry, Daddy. I didn't know where else to go. I wish I could go back in time and do things differently, but I can't. I can only apologize and move forward. Please believe me when I say I've changed."

He blinked and licked his lips. "Well, I suppose you showed good judgment in coming home at least. I'm glad I'm good for something."

Lily tensed. "Don't say that, Dad. You're the best horseman I've ever met."

He snorted. "Just not much of a father."

"That's not true. You're my father. And if I wished you away, I'd have to wish myself away because I'm a part of you and Mom. And I won't do that, no matter how bad things get."

"Sometimes we bring hardships on ourselves, girl. It's no one's fault but our own."

"Dad, I'm not a girl anymore. I'm a woman. And you're right. I've done a lot of things I regret. But now I want to start fresh. All I'm asking is for you to help me do that. I won't let you down again."

He looked startled but didn't comment. She didn't want to argue with him, not about this. She knew her father to be a man of his word. And once he told her he'd help her, she knew he meant it. But he obviously didn't like the circumstances. Neither did she.

He coughed, a deep hacking sound.

"Do you have a cold?" she asked.

"Something like that. It's getting better now."

As they passed through Emerald Valley, Lily tensed, the memory of the flood rushing through her with icy fingers. But Dad didn't take the normal route. Instead, they passed over the river on a tall Bailey bridge farther downstream.

"When did they put this up?" she asked.

"Two weeks ago. With all the flooding we've been having, the ranger made some calls. The governor contacted the Army Corps of Engineers, who brought in men to build several bridges like this so we ranchers have a safe way in and out of the valley. Even the school bus takes this route. You just didn't know about it."

"Well, I do now." And it'd be a long time before she willingly drove through the area where she'd been caught in the flash flood.

Once they passed the flood zone, she relaxed and took a moment to study Dad more closely. The pasty, leathered skin and deep creases around his eyes. The calloused hands and gray hair. She'd been gone a long time. Too long. When had her father gotten so old?

"I reckon you're planning to keep the baby, right?" he asked.

Hearing her own question voiced out loud made her pause. "I'm thinking of giving her up for adoption once she's born."

"It's a girl?"

"Yes."

"Well, I'm glad you decided not to get rid of her."

The thought made Lily stare. She could never do such a thing. She just couldn't. "Abortion was never an option for me."

"Harrumph. At least your mother and I taught you some good things, then."

A bristle of resentment shivered up her spine, but she realized what he said was true. She just didn't want to argue with him anymore. She wanted peace. "Yes, you did, Daddy. But more than that, I couldn't do such a thing. A couple of years ago, I worked with a woman who was adopted and she loved her parents."

His bushy eyebrows lifted. "Why don't you want to raise the kid yourself?"

The truck hit a pothole and Lily gripped the arm rest tight. "I don't have a father for my baby and I think kids deserve two parents, if possible. So I figured adoption was the best choice."

"Where is the dad?" Dad's voice rose slightly, but she could tell he was doing an admirable job of controlling his voracious temper.

"He…he's gone. And I wouldn't go back to him even if he asked me to."

"Why not? He was good enough to father your child. Wasn't he good enough to be a husband?"

Heat flushed her cheeks. She didn't want to tell Dad about

the abuse she'd suffered at Tommy's hands, or that he was already married with children. Knowing Dad's temper, he might hunt down Tommy and try to kill him. "No, Dad, he's not. I just need a safe place to stay until the baby's born."

"Well, I suppose I can offer you that."

Again, a blaze of gratitude speared her heart. In spite of what she'd done, the Lord had brought her safely home. He'd placed good people in her path to help her return. "Thanks, Dad."

He cleared his voice but didn't speak. How she wished he'd say something kind to her. Even that he loved her. When he'd hugged her two days ago in the clinic, it'd been the happiest—and saddest—day of her life.

"I can't say I like the idea of giving my own grandbaby away to strangers," he said.

"I still have time to think it over. It's not final."

"I don't know what there is to think over. It doesn't sit right with me to give away one of our own family members."

"I just want to do what's right for this child. I'm not abandoning her. I'm thinking about her future."

"We don't throw family away."

Was that what Lily was doing if she gave her baby up for adoption? Throwing her child away?

No, Dad didn't understand. Lily wanted her baby to be happy. It'd be so easy for her to keep the baby, but she wanted to do what the Lord desired. And because Lily had messed up her life so much, she wasn't sure at all that she was the best mother for her child.

Taking a deep breath, Lily let it go. Coming home wasn't going to be easy. She didn't want to be forced into doing something she didn't feel was right, yet she didn't want to argue with Dad, either. Thankfully they didn't need to deal with the issue today.

Chapter Four

As Dad and Lily pulled into the yard at Emerald Ranch, a black-and-white dog trotted from the barn to greet them with several loud barks. Lily looked around with interest. Everything appeared the same, except a long stable had been erected near the corrals. And the place had a slightly disorderly appearance in upkeep. A few rails had fallen off one of the fences and the gate hung on its hinges. The enormous red barn sat off to one side, needing a fresh coat of paint. So did the white house. Never in all her growing-up years had Dad ever let the blue trim reach the point of peeling.

No vegetable garden had been quartered off at the side of the house and furrowed for planting. It wasn't too late to get some seeds in the ground and Lily made a mental note to take care of that soon. Her mouth watered at the thought of home-grown tomatoes and yellow crookneck squash. She didn't say anything, but couldn't help wondering why Dad had let the place fall into disrepair.

Corrals surrounded the barn for working horses, all empty except two. A number of pretty mares and younger colts lifted their heads from a trough of hay long enough to blink at them before going back to feeding. Where was all the livestock Dad used to have around the place? The cows, horses, pigs and chickens?

He parked the truck beside the stable and got out, moving with less agility than she remembered.

"Hi, there, Beans." He ruffled the dog's ears and coughed again.

His boot heels tapped against the wooden porch. White wicker chairs sat angled to one side with a small table to rest glasses of lemonade in the evening. Lily remembered sitting here almost every day when she'd been young. Now, the chairs needed a fresh coat of paint and new cushions.

As they walked into the house, Lily was overwhelmed by the scent of pine. Memories flooded her as she gazed around the dingy room. The curtains were drawn closed. Magazines, papers and dirty dishes littered the coffee table. A thick layer of dust coated the end tables and bookshelf. From the looks of the worn carpet, it hadn't been vacuumed in some time. When had Daddy last cleaned?

He led her back to her bedroom and she was surprised to find it just as she'd left it, except for a layer of dust. The small window where she'd sat daydreaming…and used to sneak out of the house after a fight with Dad. The stuffed animals and dolls crowding her bed, which no longer held any appeal to her. The purple afghan Mom had made for her sixteenth birthday, just before she died. Lily planned to keep that forever.

Without thinking, she reached a hand up to touch Mom's large engagement ring, which she wore on a chain around her neck. Dad had given the ring to Lily the day they'd buried her mother and she'd never taken it off since. She'd thought of pawning the ring for money to take care of herself and the baby but hadn't been able to do so. The warm weight of the ring beneath her shirt gave her comfort, as though Mom were always with her, watching over her.

Lily had sure let her mother down this time. And Dad, too.

Lily didn't deserve their affection. And yet she realized they both loved her as unconditionally as she loved her unborn child. She knew now that even Dad with his irascible temper still loved her.

"Once you get settled, I'd like you to meet someone," he said.

She lifted her hands in a careless gesture. "I'm settled now, Dad. I have nothing to put away."

"Okay, then. Come on." He turned and she followed him outside to the stable.

The dog had been lying on the front porch and hopped up to pad after them, tongue lolling out of the side of his mouth.

"This is Beans?" Lily asked.

"Yep. A good cattle dog, but I haven't had much work for him lately because we no longer have any cows."

"Why not?" She walked beside Dad, having no difficulty keeping up with his ponderous stride. She remembered he used to walk so briskly.

"Um, I'm just too busy with the horses to take care of cows anymore."

She didn't believe that. Dad too busy to herd a few cows? Even if he wasn't in the market to sell them, he always raised a couple of cows for beef. But she'd been gone for years and no longer knew anything about her father's life.

She breathed deep of the fresh air, glad to be out of the stuffy house. This afternoon, she'd start scrubbing the rooms from stem to stern. Right now, she figured Dad had a ranch hand or horse trainer he wanted to introduce her to.

He slid open the wide double doors of the stable. Drafts of sunlight filtered over bales of hay stacked on one side near a small tractor. As Lily stepped inside, she caught the musty scent of straw and horses. A smell she found familiar and pleasing.

Dust motes sifted through the air. Several saddles rested on racks along one wall with tack and various tools hung neatly on hooks nearby. Stalls lined the other wall. She gazed at it with curiosity, liking the building immediately. She remembered how she'd spent hours in the barn, brushing horses, bottle feeding baby calves, or hiding up in the loft to avoid Dad's temper. Strange how much she now wanted to be back here at home.

Dad gestured toward one of the stalls far away from the mares and Lily heard the low nicker of a horse. A big sorrel stallion stood inside, a white star on his forehead. The quarterhorse lifted his proud head and took a couple of steps forward, his ears perked. Lily admired his conformation, sleek lines and wavy black mane. Dad had taught her to recognize good horseflesh when she saw it and this was a fine specimen. She could understand why Dad kept the stallion isolated from the mares. Just his presence in the stable could keep the girls agitated.

"He's beautiful," she breathed, unable to deny a shiver of delight at seeing such a lovely animal.

Dad grunted. "His name is Peg."

"Peg? That's an odd name for a stallion."

"His name's Pegasus, but I call him Peg."

Lily edged closer, extending her hand slowly, palm up. Many stallions were temperamental and she didn't want to get bit. "Is he gentle?"

"Very. A child could halter and tack him up. But he's fast. You should see him move. A winged Pegasus. Like lightning." Dad clapped his hands together and the horse jerked his head up at the sharp sound.

Peg nickered and nudged Lily's hand. She rubbed the velvety softness of his muzzle, delighted to have a new friend.

Dad chuckled. "He's after his treat."

"Treat?" Lily ran her hands over Peg's face and neck. A thrill of excitement tingled through her as she gazed into the animal's intelligent brown eyes. How she wished she could ride him.

Dad reached into his pants pocket and withdrew a single peppermint cube. He handed it to Lily. "It's not good for him, so I only give him one a day. But he loves it."

Lily stared at the peppermint resting on her open palm, stunned that Dad would surrender it to her. Peg nudged her shoulder, eager for his treat. Lily laughed and lowered her hand so the horse could nibble the candy. She wouldn't have believed it if she hadn't witnessed it with her own eyes, but after the horse swallowed, he waved his head in pleasure. A low nicker came from his throat and he nudged her arm, as if begging for more.

"Well, look at that. He's taken to you already," Dad said.

Lily blinked, unable to explain the sudden rush of emotions cascading through her. Funny how much the acceptance of a mere animal meant to her. She'd always been better with animals than with people.

Together, they patted the stallion. Sharing this special moment with her father did something to Lily. Whenever they'd worked with horses, she'd been at peace with Dad. It was their one common ground. Something they both loved and enjoyed. How she wished they could be friends in other areas of their lives, as well.

Tears fogged her vision and she turned away so Dad wouldn't see. She never used to be a crybaby, but that had been before she'd almost ruined her life. Before she'd turned her back on her father and the Lord. It wouldn't be easy, but she was determined to mend all her broken fences.

"Wait until you watch him work," Dad said. "He's quick and needs very little guidance. I trained him myself. I spent so much time with him that I almost ignored the rest of the ranch."

Was that why the place seemed in such disrepair? That

didn't make sense. If Dad was so busy, there ought to be some ranch hands around to do the other chores.

Dad jutted his chest out in pride. A pleased smile curved his mouth and Lily couldn't help wishing he'd look like that when he spoke about her. She'd just need to show him that she could be a person he could be proud of.

"Which event?" she asked.

"Reining."

"Has he won anything yet?"

Dad chuckled. "Oh, yes. It's my pleasure to introduce you to the horse that won the Limited Open Reining World Championship and the Intermediate Open Reserve World Championship two years ago."

Her mouth dropped open. Dad never kidded about things like this. "So, he's a world champion? Are you serious, Daddy?"

He glanced at her, his stern mouth barely twitching with a smile. "I certainly am."

Awe seeped through every pore in her body. Her father had a world champion reining horse living in his stable. Amazing!

"Are you boarding him? Who's his owner?"

Dad coughed again, covering his mouth with one hand. "I am, darlin'. He belongs to me."

Darlin'. He'd called her that name when she'd been young. During the few times when he'd shown her affection.

"A horse like this would also make a good cutting horse. He needs cows to chase," she said.

"You're right. Now you're here, we'll get some cows as soon as we can." He took several deep inhales, as if he couldn't catch his breath.

"Dad, are you all right?"

He lifted a hand, brushing her concerns aside. "Of course. I'm fine."

She shook her head, trying to make sense of this. "I don't understand. Where did you get Peg?"

"I bought him just after you left. His previous owner was lazy and didn't realize Peg's potential. I worked with Peg and took him to a lot of competitions. We lived on the road for almost a year, driving from event to event. Peg's a great traveler. I sold most of my livestock and hired a hand to take care of the ranch while I was gone. Peg won almost every event I entered him in, but the ranch didn't do quite so well. Remember when you called several years ago, I told you I had a sweet horse I wanted you to meet?"

No, she didn't remember, but she'd been selfish and wrapped up in herself back then.

"Well, here he is. Pegasus. The best horse I've ever seen or had the pleasure to own."

She whistled low beneath her breath, proud of her father's accomplishment. And a lot of regret that she hadn't been here to share it with him. No wonder the ranch looked run-down. Dad had been on the road with his horse. But why hadn't he fixed the ranch up since he'd returned? "To be the world champion in reining, Peg must be worth a pretty penny."

"He is. About two hundred thousand dollars worth. I've got a number of colts and fillies sired by him that I've been working with and several quality mares expecting his foals in a few months. And he's yours now."

"Mine?" Confusion filled her mind.

"If you've got the gumption to stay this time, I'll give him to you, Lily. I figure we can turn Peg to stud. Now you're here, we can build Emerald Ranch up again like it used to be when your mother was alive."

She froze, her mind racing. In spite of everything, Dad wanted her to stay. To help run the ranch. And from the looks of things, he needed her help. Badly.

His request touched her like nothing else could. And yet,

she knew it was futile to think of staying. Maybe Dad loved her in his own way but he didn't like her much. They just didn't get along. They never had. She couldn't stand to spend the rest of her life arguing with him. "But *you* can do that, Dad, can't you?"

He shook his head. "If you're not here, I have no reason to work the ranch anymore."

His words shocked her. He loved Emerald Ranch, just as she did. "But Emerald Ranch is your whole life."

"No, Lily." He looked at her, his hazel eyes piercing her to her soul. "The ranch isn't my life. You are. And now that baby you're carrying."

She'd never expected to hear such words from her father. He hadn't said he loved her, but he couldn't put his feelings more bluntly. Her heart gave a powerful squeeze.

"I've been a bit under the weather lately," he said. "I'm getting old and my body's wearing out. I just can't do it alone anymore."

Something was wrong here. Something she didn't understand. Was Daddy ailing? She'd speak with Dr. Kenner when she went in for her next prenatal appointment. He'd been the family's doctor since she was born. Hopefully he knew something about Dad's hacking cough and why he didn't seem to have as much energy anymore. And in that moment, she felt so selfish. Dad had always been here, waiting. Bigger than life. Too tough to ever die.

Or was he?

He stared at her, not quite smiling, his eyes aglow with expectancy. "Well? What do you think, darlin'? It'll take a lot of work, but once you have the baby, you can start training horses again. We can make a go of this together. Mom would be so happy if she were here."

He talked as if he expected her to stay. As if he expected

her to keep the baby. "Dad, I think we should talk about this a little more. I'm not sure I can—"

"Hello?"

Lily turned and found Nathan Coates standing behind them. His broad shoulders filled the doorway, blocking the sunlight, his warm eyes cast in shadow. The moment Lily saw him, her pulse sped up into triple time.

"Nate! I didn't expect to see you again so soon." Dad walked toward the forest ranger, his hand extended.

Lily remained where she was. Why was Nate here? If she didn't know better, she'd think the forest ranger had taken a special interest in her. Not surprising considering he'd saved her life several days ago. But she wanted to be left alone. To have time to heal her relationship with Dad and the Lord.

Obviously her father liked the man. He had a lot in common with the ranger. But Lily didn't want Nate hanging around all the time. Enough was enough.

Now, she just had to find a way to convince Nate.

Chapter Five

"Didn't mean to intrude." Nate shook Hank's hand and smiled, trying to appear casual when he felt anything but. Lily eyed him with a perturbed frown and he felt like an interloper. He shouldn't have come out here so soon, yet he felt compelled. Like an inner force was pushing him to watch out for this woman and her child.

Now he felt like a dunce.

"What do you want?" Lily asked, her dainty forehead crinkled with disapproval.

"Lily! Don't be rude," Hank said.

Nope, Nate shouldn't have come. He couldn't explain why Lily had become so important to him, or the sensations swarming his chest every time he looked into her expressive brown eyes. A man like him ought to have more control over his emotions. Some invisible force pulled him to her in spite of his resolve to stay away. He was acting like a young, lovestruck kid. And he wasn't in love. He'd know it if he were. He didn't believe in love at first sight. It took years of deep friendship and growing trust to love a woman.

Didn't it?

"I…I came to see Peg." Nate stepped farther into the stable and gazed at the stallion standing in the farthest stall.

Okay, nice recovery, if Lily bought it. Nate loved working with horses and he was good at it, too. He didn't come out to Emerald Ranch often, but when he did, he always stopped in to see the stallion.

As he reached a hand out to run his palm over the horse's left cheek, he peered at Hank. "Have you given him his candy today?"

Hank jutted his chin toward Lily. "She just gave it to him and he gobbled it down."

Nate chuckled as the horse nudged his shoulder. On occasion, Hank let him give the horse his treat. The two men had a rodeo bond. They both loved this horse and it seemed they both cared for Lily, too. "No, boy, you've had enough for today. We don't want you to get the colic."

A deep sigh of impatience whispered past Lily's lips and Nate looked at her. Her eyes narrowed on him, her expression completely hostile.

Nope, he definitely shouldn't be here.

"Well, I best be on my way. I have a few streambeds I want to check throughout the valley, to see what the flooding level is doing today. I'm planning to go up the mountain in a helicopter tomorrow afternoon." Nate stepped back, prepared to leave.

"Why a helicopter?" Lily asked.

He turned to face her, liking the way her beautiful brown eyes crinkled with curiosity. "With three bridges out in Ruby Valley, I called the regional Forest Service office in Ogden, Utah, for help. Because of our serious flood situation, we're the only ones in the region they've allowed to use a helicopter. I plan to fly across the East Humboldt area and the Ruby Mountains. We'll look for any debris dams that are building up in front of a potential flood. It's the best way to be aware so we can prepare for danger down below."

Her brow furrowed. "What kind of danger?"

"Debris torrents. They move fast, usually strike without warning, and destroy property and kill anything in their path."

Hank scratched his chin. "You mean like a mudslide?"

Nate shook his head. "No, a debris torrent is caused by boulders, tree limbs and rootwads that dam up in places like narrow canyons and ravines. The melt-off from heavy snows or rains builds up behind it. When it breaks loose, the destructive force is astounding. It can come down the mountain at speeds above thirty-five miles per hour. It obliterates anything in its path, including a ranch house. I've seen the devastation it leaves behind afterward, and it's serious. I want to take a look and see if we've got any of our ranches in danger."

"Ah, I've lived in this valley all my life and never seen anything like that here," Hank said.

"It could still happen," Nate said. "The snowpack we've had this past winter beats anything on record to date. We've probably had a one-hundred-and-fifty-year winter."

Lily rested a hand atop her round stomach. "What do you mean by that?"

"The snows we had this winter probably come only once every one hundred and fifty years. It's just not normal. I don't want to be an alarmist, but I want us to take precautions if the excess melt-off might cause a debris torrent to come down on one of our ranchers."

"Bah! We'll be just fine." Hank waved a hand in the air, brushing Nate off.

Lily didn't look so convinced. Her tiny nose crinkled with her frown. "Do you think Emerald Ranch is in danger?"

At first glance, she looked relaxed, her voice casual, but Nate knew better. He heard the slight catch in her voice and knew his admonition worried her. And he didn't want this woman to fret about anything except having a healthy baby. "Not yet, but I'll be flying up tomorrow and then again in a couple of weeks, just to make sure."

"I'd like to go with you, if that's possible."

Nate coughed, surprised by her request. But then he realized she was motivated to protect Emerald Ranch, not be near him. He glanced at her stomach, then up to the butterfly bandage covering the small gash on her forehead. A feeling of warmth and protectiveness blanketed him. If he did anything to cause her to lose her baby, he'd never forgive himself. "You can come along, but only if your doctor says it's okay."

"I can call Dr. Kenner's office today, but I should be okay to fly for a couple more months. I feel fine. And the baby moves all the time."

Nate would love to feel the baby's movements. How he wished he had a right to press his palm against her stomach and feel the little kicks there. The thought of spending the afternoon with her appealed to Nate, no denying it. "Good. I'll swing by to pick you up around noon tomorrow."

"Okay." She turned and walked toward the house, her long hair bouncing with her brisk stride.

With her gone, Hank clasped Nate's upper arm. "Look, Nate, I really like you, but I don't want you to get Lily all worked up over nothing. She just got home and I don't want to worry her. Not with a baby on the way."

Nate nodded. "I agree, but I don't think it's wise to keep her in the dark, either. She has a right to know the dangers, in case she needs to get herself away from the ranch in a hurry. I wouldn't tell you about debris torrents if I didn't think they were something to take very seriously. Hopefully nothing will come of this, but if it does, I hope you'll trust my judgment."

Nate walked away, giving Hank no opportunity to argue. Nate knew what he was doing. If he didn't go up on the mountain and then warn the ranchers of potential hazards, they could blame the Forest Service. Nate had to do everything in his power to ensure that didn't happen. But his concern for Lily went even deeper. He'd saved her and her child's life from a flash flood and he wasn't about to see her harmed by something even worse.

The whir of the helicopter blades overhead stirred up a dust cloud around the tarmac at the small airport just outside of Jasper. Lily shielded her eyes against the afternoon sun and waited beside Nate while the chopper landed. She'd called the doctor the day before and he'd signed a note saying she could go up in the air if she felt well. She should avoid flying in a big airliner after eight months.

"Come on." Nate cupped her elbow and led her out onto the blacktop. The sliding door of the chopper opened and Nate helped her step up inside before greeting the pilot.

"Howdy. I'm Eddie Slater." The pilot reached across the seat to shake Nate's hand.

"I'm Nate Coates and this is Lily Hansen, one of our local ranchers. Thanks for flying in to help with this project."

Eddie's gaze lowered to the gentle bulge of Lily's stomach and his eyes widened. The pilot looked doubtful, but before he could speak, Nate interceded. "She has a release from her doctor to fly."

Eddie's expression softened and he turned back to his controls. "Okay, if you say so."

Lily sat back and buckled her seat belt. Nate did the same, his warm gaze resting on her face. "You okay?"

She nodded, hoping he didn't get the wrong idea. She hadn't tagged along because she was interested in him. "I'm just worried about Emerald Ranch. I want to make sure we're not in danger."

He flashed a consoling smile. "Me, too."

Did he really care, or was this just the forest ranger talking?

As the chopper lifted off, Lily gazed out the window, concentrating on the ground below. She would have gone online last night to check out more info on debris torrents, but Dad didn't own a computer or have an internet connection at the ranch. If she decided to stay here, she'd have to remedy that.

She'd never heard of anything but a flash flood, and she couldn't imagine the kind of damage Nate had described. On the evening news several years earlier, she recalled seeing the damage mudslides had caused to some homes in California. But here in sleepy Jasper, Nevada, she couldn't imagine something like a debris torrent taking out an entire ranch.

Eddie flew the helicopter over town and then toward the mountains. In the lower valleys, pools of water surrounded green fields of alfalfa. The chopper skirted the side of long stretches of road where a narrow bridge of six-inch layers of asphalt stood with no support underneath. Lily had never seen anything like it before.

"Did the floods cause that?" she asked.

"Yep, the water was so intense that it just swept away the base beneath the road," Nate said. "You can see why we've closed it off. It looks innocent enough, but a car passing along that road wouldn't realize the danger until it's too late. The weight of the car would collapse the bridge of asphalt and cause serious injury to the driver."

Lily shook her head in awe, wondering how Nate knew about these things. His expertise and caution on behalf of the community impressed her.

Within minutes, the chopper climbed high into the Ruby Mountains where twenty-foot poles had been set up to measure the depths of snow. Nate lifted a pair of binoculars to his eyes before scanning the area with his gaze.

"Where are the poles? I can't see a single one." Lily squinted out the window.

"That's because they're all buried beneath the snow."

Eddie gave a low whistle. "That means the snow is over

twenty-feet deep here. And it's the end of April. Even with the level of melt-off and flooding you've been having, I don't think the floods are finished yet."

"Me, either," Nate agreed.

This revelation amazed Lily. "How many feet of snow did we get this year?"

"We estimate over thirty-three feet. In February, we had to bring in dump trucks and front-end loaders to clear the snow away from Main Street in town just so cars could drive through."

Eddie steered the chopper away from the enormous white drifts, following the rivulets of melt-off as they ran into the nearby creeks. The chopper followed the headwaters leading down the mountain to the valleys below. The runoff started out small, but quickly became rushing torrents of water.

Near Secret Valley, Lily gasped. A geyser sprayed outward from the mountain, taking them all by surprise. It came from nowhere, reminding her of a broken fire hydrant she'd seen in Houston, spraying high into the air before splashing down below and soaking everything in sight. The kids had played in the water before the fire department had shut it down.

"Where is that much water coming from?" Lily asked.

Nate didn't look at her as he answered. He seemed to be studying the erosion caused by the vast stream. "Underground streams inside the mountain. Most people don't realize we have tunnels of rivers flowing beneath the ground. When those underground rivers can't hold the water, they explode outward."

Lily felt impressed by his knowledge. "I never knew."

He pointed at a steep ravine leading downstream. "Look at that."

Eddie lowered the chopper so they could get a better look. Entire uprooted trees, rootwads, boulders and mountains of dirt blocked the flow of the melt-off. Rushing water had started backing up behind the dam, caught in the narrow canyon with nowhere else to go.

Nowhere but down the mountain.

"Wow! That dam must be twenty-feet high," Eddie exclaimed.

"At least." Nate turned his head to look at Lily. "This is what I was trying to describe to you and Hank. This is the beginning of a debris torrent."

"But where did all those dead trees come from?"

"About ten years after timber is cut, the roots of the trees decompose. Heavy rains and snow push the dirt and rootwads down into the ravines below where they cause debris dams. That's why I shut down timber harvest here in this area of the mountain after I arrived in Jasper. We can use our natural resources, but we need to manage them effectively so they don't create a worse problem. This area has been overharvested for trees, causing erosion."

Lily widened her eyes. Never before had she realized the full impact of what humankind did to cause mayhem to the environment. She was now a believer. She had to tell Dad about this. Because she'd seen it with her own eyes, he'd surely believe her. "Is Emerald Ranch safe?"

They flew over the mountain ridges above the ranch. From this distance, she got a great view of the house, barn, green fields and corrals with frolicking colts and fillies. Absolutely stunning in its beauty.

Lily held her breath and awaited Nate's verdict.

"I don't see anything yet," he finally said.

Yet! Lily released her breath in a slow exhale. "Do you think that could change?"

"Yes, it could. I'll fly up here again in two weeks, just to make sure nothing develops in the meantime."

What a relief. Knowing Nate was here to watch over the ranch gave Lily a sense of security she hadn't felt in years.

"But what will happen with the debris dam we saw above Bill Stokely's place?"

Nate swiveled around to stare out the window again. "With all the pressure the water behind the dam is creating, the Stokelys better watch out if it ever breaks loose."

Eddie shook his head. "I'd sure hate to find myself in the middle of its path."

Lily agreed. "Can the dam be dissolved somehow, so it won't be a danger to Bill and his family?"

Nate shook his head. "Nope. There's no way to remove the dam without it giving way. But Bill can move until the flood waters have absorbed into the earth and dried out."

That wasn't what any rancher wanted to hear. No man wanted to lose his ranch. It was his home and livelihood. But Lily figured moving his livestock and family was better than losing their lives.

"We will have to go down and warn them." Nate pointed toward the valley floor.

The chopper headed down the mountain, following the route the flood would take if it should break through the dam. Wide fields opened to their view, surrounding the barn and house of the Stokelys' place. Even here, the irrigation ditches had overflowed, flooding the alfalfa so the brown Angus cattle huddled together in dry corners as they grazed. Emerald Ranch was in the same predicament, except they didn't have any cattle to worry about.

Just world championship quarterhorses.

"Can you set the chopper down in that empty field over there?" Nate pointed to a dry area uninhabited by livestock.

"You bet." Eddie did as told. Within minutes, the chopper bumped down, but Eddie didn't kill the engine in case it wouldn't start up again. Better to leave it running on idle.

"You want to go with me to speak with Bill Stokely?" Nate asked Lily.

"Would my presence help?"

"I think so."

She nodded, not wanting to miss any piece of this operation. "I've known Bill and Myra Stokely all my life. Myra was my mom's best friend. I hate that their ranch is in danger."

"We won't be very long," Nate told Eddie as he slid open the door and hopped down. He helped Lily out and together they walked briskly toward the house. Even then, she could tell Nate had slowed his stride so she could keep up.

The barking of dogs heralded their arrival and Bill Stokely came out of the wide, log house. He stood on the front porch wearing blue coveralls and a red kerchief. A speck of bread stuck to the corner of his mouth, indicating he must have been inside having lunch.

When they were within hearing distance, Bill called out, "Well, hi there, Lily."

"Hi, Bill!" She waved.

He stepped forward and hugged her, showing a welcoming smile. "I heard you were back in town. It's sure good to see you, honey. Although you've grown a bit."

His gray eyes twinkled as he indicated her pregnancy, but she saw no censure there. Did he know she wasn't married?

"And you, too," she replied.

"Myra! Lily Hansen's here," Bill called to the house.

"Oh, my goodness. It's little Lily." The screen door clapped closed behind Myra as she came outside.

Lily found herself engulfed in a bevy of hugs and kisses. Except for grayer hair and more wrinkles, Myra still had the same rosy cheeks and strong, lean body. In fact, Lily couldn't remember ever seeing a fat rancher's wife. They worked too hard.

Myra stood back and looked Lily up and down with approval. "And we're gonna have a baby. How wonderful. I've got some new little quilts and booties I just knitted this past winter. Oh, won't we have fun dressing this little one?"

"Thanks, Myra." Tears misted Lily's eyes. Except for the disappointment over her lack of marriage, Lily could almost imagine her own mother would have greeted her the same way. Maybe she did have some allies here in Jasper after all.

"I didn't expect to see you today." Bill's smile faded and he spoke in a gruff voice as he eyed Nate.

From past disagreements over grazing permits and water rights, Lily knew Bill didn't like the Forest Service much. It seemed that sentiment hadn't changed. But Lily couldn't blame Nate for doing his job. Right now, the ranchers needed the forest ranger. Very much.

"I thought I'd pay you a visit." Nate's voice sounded pleasant considering the news he was bringing with him.

Myra linked her arm with Lily's and they waited, listening carefully to what was said.

Bill jerked a thumb toward the helicopter. "What're you doing out here in that machine?"

Without mincing words, Nate quickly explained about the debris jam they'd just seen up in the mountains.

"One of the dams is right above your place." Nate pointed toward a stand of tall aspen skirting the west side of the ranch and everyone turned to look. From this distance, the mountain looked harmless enough. "I just wanted to warn you, Bill. I suggest you move your livestock and family to higher ground. If that debris torrent gives way, it'll sweep through your house like a broom on an insect. You won't have much warning."

Bill pursed his lips. "Nonsense. Nothing short of an earthquake could do that much damage to my ranch."

"Believe me, it could." Nate's voice sounded serious. He meant what he said.

"Nothing like that's ever happened here before," Bill returned.

"It's not frequent, but I've seen it," Nate continued. "And you don't want to be down here if it happens."

From her peripheral vision, Lily saw Nate shift his weight. He didn't show any emotion, but his shoulders tensed with urgency. He must really want the Stokelys to move.

"I think we'll stay right here."

"Look, Bill, I can't legally haul you off your place, but I've got to document this warning as soon as I get back to my office. If I were a rancher, I'd rather have my family safe than sorry."

Bill folded his arms and gave Nate a condescending smile. "I appreciate the warning. You do what you gotta do, Ranger. But I'm not worried. My dad was ranching here long before we had any forest rangers telling us what to do. Besides, I'm insured by an Agripak farm and ranch policy. I've seen lots of floods during my time and we'll be okay."

Bill's voice dripped with disdain, but Nate didn't react in anger. He merely nodded with respect. "I understand."

Lily couldn't deny a feeling of appreciation for what Nate was trying to do. If Bill decided not to heed the warnings, that was Bill's problem. But Lily still didn't like the thought of someone being killed because Bill was too foolish to listen to reason.

"I wonder if we have insurance," Lily said.

"You should ask your dad," Nate replied. "The last time I saw a debris torrent take out someone's ranch, the insurance policy wouldn't cover the damage. It had several exclusions and didn't cover water or land movements. Be sure to check it out as soon as possible."

She nodded, feeling troubled.

The low murmur of the helicopter engine reminded them that Eddie was waiting for them.

"We best be on our way," Nate said.

"I'll be over to visit you in a day or two," Myra hugged

Lily. "I want to hear all about what you've been up to. Maybe we'll plan a shopping trip into Reno to buy some things for the baby. Oh, we'll have such a great time."

That would be so much fun under different circumstances. But until Lily decided to keep the baby, she didn't want to buy a lot of cute clothes and toys that would make her want to hold on to her child even more than she already did. "You come over anytime."

"Give my regards to your dad." Bill nodded to Lily.

"I will, thanks."

After she and Nate returned to the chopper and climbed inside, Eddie lifted the bird into the air. Lily stared down at Bill and Myra standing on the ground, growing smaller by the moment. The seat creaked as Lily sat back and breathed with relief. Emerald Ranch wasn't in danger, but if that changed in the future, she'd convince Dad to leave. She hoped he wouldn't be as mule-headed as Bill. Maybe Dad could convince the Stokelys to move for a while. These ranchers stuck together and were stubborn to the core. Probably because they had to be to survive.

"You doing okay?" Nate asked, his eyes creased with concern.

She nodded as heat flooded her face. Physically, yes, she was great. But fear of what might happen in the future made her stomach churn. She told herself there was no sense getting upset now. If a debris jam started above Emerald Ranch, they'd deal with it later.

As her gaze swept over Nate's drab olive-green ranger's shirt and gold shield, she admitted silently to herself that she was grateful he was here. Growing up, she'd never heard of any forest rangers going to such lengths to protect the ranchers. Other than Dad, Nate was the first man in her life to go out of his way to ensure she was safe, which confused her and made her suspicious of his motives.

She'd sure feel better come August, when this flooding stage had passed and she'd decided what to do about her sweet baby girl.

Chapter Six

Two busy weeks passed without Nate being able to find an excuse to visit Lily again. Two long weeks that left him feeling hollow inside.

He missed Lily. And he didn't know why.

When it came time for him to drive through the valley ranches again, Nate couldn't deny a feeling of excitement. If he asked, would Lily agree to a date with him this Friday night?

Yeah, that was wishful thinking on his part.

As usual, Nate found Hank and his daughter working out in the stable. Hank smiled and shook Nate's hand while Lily turned away and seemed to ignore him.

"We were just getting ready to go into the house for lunch. I'd take it as a personal favor if you'd join us," Hank said.

The insistent tone in his voice and subtle pressure on his arm told Nate the man wouldn't take no for an answer. And truthfully, Nate didn't want to leave yet. Even with Lily glaring at him like a vulture ready to pick out his eyes.

"You got something on your mind you want to discuss?" Nate asked, highly aware of Lily shifting impatiently. His gaze swept over her baby bump, which had noticeably grown. Without another word, she turned and headed back toward the house. He admired the jaunty swing of her hips. She wasn't waddling yet, but he figured it was just a matter of time.

Hank pulled Nate with him as he followed his daughter. "As a matter of fact, I do have a couple of questions for you. First, I want to make sure the Bailey bridge you had installed over Cross Creek is gonna hold up under all this flooding."

"Yeah, it'll hold." Nate's boot heels crunched against the graveled driveway. "And I had one of my men put signage along the road to direct people away from the creek bed where Lily got hit by the flash flood."

He enjoyed the bounce of her soft curls as she stepped up onto the front porch of the house. She wasn't a big woman, but she had spunk, and he liked that. A lot.

She didn't wait for them at the door but went inside, the screen door clapping closed behind her.

With Lily out of earshot, Nate paused and faced Hank. "I don't think I should come in, Hank. You and your daughter need time alone. Don't worry about the Bailey bridge. It'll hold."

Hank clasped Nate's arm. "Don't go. I don't mean to cut into your work time, but I really wish you'd take a meal with us. I owe you big time for saving Lily, but I also have another favor to ask you...." A deep, hard cough shook Hank's chest and he almost doubled over with the force of it.

The back screen door flew open and Lily rushed down the steps to her father's side. "Daddy, are you okay?"

She wrapped an arm around her father's back, supporting him until the coughing spasm subsided. Gut-wrenching fear filled her eyes and that's when Nate realized how much she loved her father. It couldn't be easy having an irascible man like Hank Hansen for a dad and Nate's heart warmed toward her.

"I...I'm fine." Hank gasped for breath.

"I don't like this cough you've got, Dad. I think we need to go back into town to see the doctor again."

Hank drew away and brushed off her concern. "I told you I already saw Doc Kenner before you came home. I've got some medicine in the house. I'll take it and be fine."

Without a backward glance, the older man reached for the door. "Come on, you two. I'm frying bacon for BLT sandwiches. You can both help. I'm starved. Let's eat."

Nate stood where he was, gazing at Lily's dubious expression. "I'm sorry, Lily. I know you don't want me here."

Okay, maybe he was being a bit blunt. But at the age of thirty-two, he was too old to play games with a pretty woman. And he still didn't have a handle on his feelings for her. She obviously didn't like him. But what he couldn't understand was why he liked her so much.

She faced him squarely. "Let's get one thing straight right now, cowboy. I'm not interested in you. Not now, not ever. Okay?"

He grit his teeth, wondering who had hurt her so badly that she seemed to dislike men so much. "What gives you the idea I'm interested in you?"

She pursed her lips. "It's obvious."

He arched one brow, trying not to laugh at the way her face crinkled with repugnance. "How so?"

She lifted a hand and jutted her chin. "Because you keep showing up here."

"Don't flatter yourself, Lily. I've got a job to do. Part of that includes doing what I can to ensure no one else gets hurt. The Forest Service doesn't need a bunch of lawsuits because I didn't build enough Bailey bridges or warn the ranchers. I thought after our helicopter ride you understood that."

"Oh." She frowned as if the idea of suing the government hadn't occurred to her. "I'd never sue you. It wasn't anyone's fault I got hit by that flash flood. I'm lucky to be alive."

"I'm glad you feel that way, but I'm also glad you and your baby are okay."

She shifted her weight, resting a hand against her hip. "I don't mean to sound ungrateful, Nate. Really I don't. You've been a big help and I appreciate what you're doing to help the ranchers. It's only that my life is complicated right now. I don't have room in my life for another man. I can't afford the heartache. Not with a baby on the way. As long as you understand and accept that, we'll get along fine."

Her candor made him furious at the jerk who had cankered her toward men. She'd obviously been hurt. Badly. And the way Nate was feeling right now, he'd be happy to knock the guy out with one punch.

"You're talking about Tommy." A statement, not a question.

Her eyes widened with shock. "How do you know his name?"

"When I drove you to the clinic, you were in and out of consciousness. You said his name." He didn't add that she'd cried Tommy's name with fear and dread. At the time, Nate hadn't fully understood who Tommy was or what the man had done, but he knew the type.

A worthless, no-good piece of rat bait. The kind of rubbish that gave honorable men a bad name.

"That doesn't change anything between you and me. I'm not interested. Got it?" She paused, giving Nate time to absorb her words. Her eyes drilled into his like a high-powered tool.

"Okay, I got it. But you should know I'm not interested in you romantically, either." At least he didn't think he was. He figured if he said it out loud enough times, he might stop thinking about her all the time.

"Good. We understand each other, then." She gave a sharp nod.

"We do. Now can we be friends?"

Her beautiful eyes narrowed. "I don't think so."

A derisive laugh slipped from his chest. "Yeah, you're right. You probably have too many friends already and don't need another one."

She froze like stone. "Maybe we *could* be friends, but nothing more."

He ignored that. "Have you seen the doctor recently?"

"I have another prenatal checkup in two weeks. Don't worry. Except for a bad case of heartburn, I'm doing fine. And the baby is a little whirling dervish. She moves often." She rubbed her stomach and showed a stiff smile.

He chuckled. "I'm glad to hear it."

"Now come in for lunch." She turned, as if she hadn't just read him the riot act.

Shaking his head in confusion, Nate followed her into the kitchen, then sat at the table. He felt useless, watching her wash off the counters, then slice lettuce and tomatoes for the sandwiches. Hank stood in front of the stove layering long slices of bacon in a pan. The meat sizzled as it hit the heat. The air smelled like morning breakfast.

No one spoke. Hank and Lily worked side-by-side, like this was an everyday occurrence. Nate fidgeted with the salt and pepper shakers for several minutes, then decided if he was going to be friends with these people, he had a right to help out. Standing, he washed his hands first, then searched the cupboards for plates and glasses to set the table. Lily glanced at him, but said nothing.

"What are we drinking?" he asked.

"The milk's in the fridge." Hank didn't look up as he used a pair of tongs to turn the bacon.

Nate retrieved a gallon of milk and poured each one of them a tall glass while Lily cored and sliced apples to lay on each of their plates.

"Can you reach the mayonnaise?" Lily asked him as she spread slices of white bread across the counter.

Nate found the jar inside the fridge door and handed it to her. Her fingers brushed against his and warmth tingled up his arm. Lily jerked back as if she'd been burned and dropped the jar. With fast reflexes, Nate caught the bottle in midair.

"That was a close one." He smiled down at her.

Standing close to Lily, their gazes met, then locked. With her tummy bumping gently against his side, he felt the unmistakable kicks of the baby and he widened his eyes in surprise. Lily's cheeks flooded a pretty pink color before she snapped the jar out of his hands and whirled around to the counter. He stood there like a mannequin for several moments, watching her slap mayonnaise on the bread with a butter knife.

Just friends. Yeah, right.

But he wondered how long she'd fight the obvious attraction between them. Confusion radiated through Nate's brain. He'd just felt her baby moving. Something intimate and entirely personal. Obviously Lily had felt the electric current between them, too, but she didn't like it.

She didn't like him.

Maybe she still loved her child's father. Maybe she hoped the man would come for her. And yet, deep down, Nate realized something more was going on here that he didn't understand.

"Pretty ring." He nodded at a large diamond ring hanging from a silver chain around her neck.

Lily looked down at the glittering bauble, then whisked the chain into hiding beneath her shirt. "It was my mother's."

"Ah, no wonder you wear it around your neck. It must mean a lot to you." He admitted to himself that he was glad Tommy hadn't given the ring to her.

She tossed him a glare. "It does."

As they sat at the table, Lily folded her arms and paused

until the two men followed suit. She closed her eyes and offered a quick blessing on the food. When she finished, she picked up a slice of apple with her dainty fingers, took a bite and ignored her father's surprised look.

"When did you get religious?" he asked.

"You and Mom taught me, remember?" She chewed and looked away.

"But I didn't think what we taught you ever took. Before you left home, you said you didn't believe in God."

"Things change. There's a lot you don't know about me anymore, Daddy. God is the only person I believe in anymore. The only one I fully trust."

Her words sank deep into Nate's mind. The conviction in her voice expressed her faith, but a lot of cynicism, too. Nate hadn't exercised his faith in a long time. Maybe it was time to remember God and all the good things in his life.

A subtle smile curved Hank's lips. "I'm glad to hear that, darlin'. It'll be nice to take you to church Sunday. I've sat alone for many years now. I'm sure lots of your old friends will be pleased to see you again."

Lily's shoulders tensed. "That might not be a good idea, Dad. I don't know if I want to see anyone yet."

Her hand slid across her abdomen and Hank's gaze dipped there before he blinked in understanding. Nate couldn't blame her for wanting to hide out here at the ranch. She was obviously embarrassed to have people in town find out she was expecting a child out of wedlock. He waited, hoping Hank might say something encouraging to her. Something loving and forgiving.

"There's no one in town who'd dare cast the first stone at my girl," Hank said.

Not exactly what Nate would call encouraging, but probably the best a gruff man like Hank Hansen could manage.

Nate cleared his voice, hoping what he said didn't offend

anyone. "All it takes is some heavy trials to remind us that we each need the Lord in our lives. Maybe that's why God tests us so often. To humble us so we'll turn to Him for help."

She looked at him like he'd just sprouted horns. Then her expression softened. "I never thought of it that way, but I'm afraid I brought this trial on myself."

"It's nothing you can't fix. You can always start fresh," Nate added. "Not everyone in town will be judgmental."

Her brown eyes flashed with resentment. Nate realized he'd said too much. An outsider who had no right to give Lily advice or participate in this conversation at her kitchen table.

Ducking his head, Nate bit into a thick sandwich and chewed, trying to fight off the whirl of thoughts filling his mind. Thoughts that would bring him nothing but trouble if he let them take hold of him. He wanted to know this woman better. To find out what made her tick. Where she'd been the past years and who had hurt her. Where was the father of Lily's baby and why wasn't he here apologizing to her now? The guy could show up any day now to claim Lily and her child.

It's what Nate would do if Lily were his. He'd never abandon her or their child.

Again, the urge to hightail it away from this ranch as soon as he could filled Nate's mind. He'd leave for a time, but he knew he'd return. And he didn't understand why. None of this made any sense. Not at all.

Why wouldn't he leave?

Lily tilted her head and stared at her plate, eating half a sandwich before she lost her appetite. She didn't mind Nate dropping by to keep them apprised of what was going on with the floods, but moving around her kitchen like he belonged there was a bit much. She'd been blunt enough, yet Nate insisted they be friends.

Not a good idea.

"Now that Lily's home, we're making plans for Peg," Hank said.

"What plans?" Nate asked.

"We're gonna build Emerald Ranch into a breeding and performance horse business. Like it was back when her momma was still alive. Lily's gonna help."

Lily jerked her head up and stared at her father. "Dad, we talked about this. I told you I may not—"

"Don't worry." He raised a hand to shush her. "I'm very aware of your delicate condition. You can't ride yet, but there's lots we can do before the baby comes."

Nate gave a half smile. "I'm glad you have plans, Hank. I always said it's a shame to let Peg grow fat inside that stall. Because he's won the world championship, you could make a tidy sum if you put him to stud."

Hank nodded, his face exploding into a wide grin. "That's my plan. It might take us some time, but now Lily's here, we're gonna make it work. I've got a grandbaby to think about."

"Dad! I told you I was thinking of giving the baby up for adoption."

Hank didn't even blink. "Nonsense. This is your home and we're a family. It's where you and the baby belong, darlin'."

Panic shivered down Lily's spine. Dad just kept ignoring what she was saying. If she fought him on this, he might throw her out of the house. And she hated discussing the issue in front of Nate.

Dad turned to face him. "Nate, you're a great hand with a horse. You really get inside their heads. I've seen you work. You did a great job training that new horse of yours to compete in the regional cutting competitions. I've got several good quarterhorses out in my corrals, but I haven't been able to break or train them because…because…I haven't had the time."

Or because he physically couldn't do it anymore? He was just too stubborn to admit any kind of weakness. For the past two weeks, Lily had watched her father work, struggling to catch his breath. Barely able to lift a bale of hay. He'd insisted he just had a bad cold, but it never seemed to get any better.

"With my instructions, Lily could train the horses," Dad continued without missing a beat. "She's that good."

"She is, huh?" Nate gazed at Lily, as if assessing her for the truth of Hank's words.

"Wait 'til you see her work. But she can't jeopardize the baby by being bucked off. Would you be willing to break and train the horses for us, Nate? Just until Lily can ride again?"

A blaze of heat rushed through Lily's face. She couldn't believe this was happening. Like always, Dad was making plans for her life. Trying to control her. Which was why she'd left in the first place.

"Dad, I don't know if I want to do this."

"What are you talking about?" Hank boomed and Lily flinched. "This is your home. Your heritage. Everything I own in the world will one day be yours. Of course you want to be a part of it. You love working with horses as much as I do. What's gotten into you, girl?"

Lily felt the blood drain from her face even as hot needles of fear prickled her skin. The room seemed to close in on her, like it did whenever Tommy had gotten angry at her. She glanced around the kitchen, looking for a place to hide. A place of refuge. Tears burned the backs of her eyes, but she blinked, refusing to let them fall. Why couldn't she just have a rational conversation with her father? Just once, she wished he'd listen to her. And try to understand.

"Lily, are you okay?" Nate asked, his voice soft.

"Yes. Fine." No! she wanted to yell. A part of her felt guilty for planning to leave because she didn't want to go. She would love to stay at Emerald Ranch forever. But she couldn't take

Dad's volatile temper. Every time she disagreed with him, he blew his cork.

"Men and women all over the country are looking for good rodeo animals." Dad ignored her. "Our horses come from excellent stock. We just need to train them and find the buyers."

"Dad, I won't—"

"Hush, girl! Of course you will." Hank turned and kept talking to Nate.

Whether it was the hormones from her pregnancy or years of enduring a man's foul temper, Lily couldn't take this right now.

With a huff of exasperation, she threw her napkin down on the table and scraped her chair back. Nate and Hank jerked their heads up in unison.

"I want no part of this," she said. "I'm this baby's mother and I'll decide what I do with my own child. I won't be forced into anything by you. I won't!"

Without another word, she whisked her dishes into the sink and walked down the hallway. She closed her bedroom door with a soft click. No slamming door. No screaming or yelling. Just a quiet dismissal.

At the age of twenty-five, Lily was now a grown woman. Way too old to be told what to do by her father. She had her own child to think about. An innocent life that took priority over everything else. Even if that meant giving her sweet baby up for adoption.

And yet, it wasn't that simple. Lily had come here, depending on Dad to help get her through this difficult time. He'd taken her in and she was beholden to him. As destitute as she was, she couldn't afford to push her father aside. She loved him. She cared about him. But she couldn't let herself get sucked back into her old life, either.

And why not?

The thought came unbidden to her brain. Why couldn't

she stay? She loved Emerald Ranch. Loved working with the horses. And Dad had offered to hand her ownership of a world championship reining horse just for sticking around. She'd done nothing to earn that right. No feeding, riding, cleaning manure from stalls or training of Peg. While she'd been off living a wild life with a married man, Dad had stayed here and kept the ranch going. Yet he was willing to hand it all over to her.

If she'd just stay.

Another layer of guilt rested across her heart. Dad needed her. She couldn't stay, yet she couldn't leave.

The mattress creaked as she sat down and reached up to clasp her mother's engagement ring through her shirt.

"What should I do, Lord?" She prayed out loud, her voice a soft quiver.

She patted her stomach and a little foot thumped against her palm. Then she felt a sense of calm pass over her.

"Don't worry, sweetheart. I'll do what's right for you." She rarely spoke out loud to the baby, forcing herself not to become too attached to the child she planned to give up for adoption. But it hadn't worked at all. She loved this baby more than her own life.

The peaceful feeling that enveloped Lily gave her the answer she sought. God wouldn't let her down. As long as she sought Him out and tried to do what was right, He would guide her. She had to have faith.

Standing, she walked over to the window where she gazed at the corrals outside.

Her child's birthright.

Lily sighed and shook her head. She didn't want to be co-erced into doing things she didn't want to do. And she definitely didn't want to be friends with Nathan Coates.

Or did she...

Chapter Seven

After Lily walked away, Nate stared at her empty chair. Obviously she didn't approve of Hank's plan. She wanted to give her baby up for adoption. And that filled Nate's mind with more questions. Like why she didn't want to raise her own child.

Hank leaned his elbows on the table and scowled, his sandwich forgotten. "I'll never understand that girl. Or her mother, either. Never as long as I live."

Hank muttered to himself, but Nate understood the confusion. He was feeling much the same way. He shouldn't care what was bothering Lily, but he did.

"So what about it?" Hank urged.

"What about what?"

"Will you work with my quarterhorses?"

"Hank, you need a real horse trainer, not me."

"You are a real trainer. A good one. I'll give you stock in the venture. You'd be well compensated for your work, Nate."

"You can train your own horses, Hank. You did a great job with Peg."

Hank lowered his head, seeming to study the green linoleum. "I know how to train horses, but I can't do it anymore, Nate. I...I'm sick."

A long pause followed while Nate digested this information. Was this the truth, or was Hank trying to play on his sympathy? "Is it serious?"

"Nah! It's nothing, really. But I can't work like I used to. I can't train the horses."

Even though Hank tried to downplay his physical condition, Nate wasn't fooled. Nothing but a serious ailment would keep Hank from working with his animals. "What's wrong with you?"

Hank heaved a labored sigh of disgust. "My ticker's wearing out. I'd rather not go into more detail than that."

"Have you seen the doctor?"

Hank's cheeks mottled with embarrassment. As if he should be able to control this weakness. "Yeah, I had a battery of tests about eight months ago. That's when I quit smoking. I just need to take it a bit easier. But now I've got to think about Lily and my grandbaby. I had forced myself to cut back so I could last long enough for Lily to come home. Now she's here, I've got to convince her to stay. I don't want to see my place sold at auction. It belongs to Lily now. Her inheritance. She doesn't know it yet, but she's the only name in my will. I'm telling you this in confidence, though. You've got to promise me you won't tell Lily I'm sick."

"Okay, I promise." Nate figured Lily would find out soon enough on her own. All you had to do was look at Hank to see he wasn't feeling well. The colorless skin. The gasping breaths. The hacking cough. It all made sense now. But Nate hadn't realized it was so severe.

"So you can see why I need your help. I'm out of options," Hank said.

"Why not hire some hands to help out on the place? You used to employ Deeter Smith. He's good at caring for horses, although he's not a trainer."

"Yeah, Deeter's dependable, too. But I…I've had some financial setbacks. I can't afford to pay an extra hand right now. That's why I thought you might be willing to help out in return for stock in the venture. I could really use your help, Nate."

"Is your illness terminal?"

Hank pursed his lips, as if reluctant to answer. Then he nodded his head once. "Afraid so. Which is one more reason you mustn't tell Lily. She's got enough worries without mollycoddling her old man."

Nate agreed, but in fairness to Lily, he figured she ought to know the truth. "How long can you live?"

"Indefinitely, if I cut back on work and take care of myself. I'm trying to do that, but it's difficult."

Nate snorted. "So I suspect bacon on your sandwich should be taboo."

"Cholesterol isn't my problem. Heart failure is."

High cholesterol caused a lot of heart problems, but it wasn't Nate's place to lecture Hank. And Lily didn't know about it. Not yet.

Scooting back, Nate stood and picked up his plate before carrying it to the sink. He paused, staring out the window as he thought over what Hank had said. "The problem is, I've got a career, Hank. I really don't have any extra time. You know I work a lot of long hours as the forest ranger. And we're coming into summer wildfire season."

Hank gave a harsh laugh. "I'll take any help you can offer. I've got prime horseflesh. Not like that scrubby stuff the other ranchers own."

True. Nate's fingers almost itched at the thought of working with quality horses again. "But flooding causes all sorts of other problems. Campgrounds and roads need to be rebuilt before the summer tourist season. I've got to check the damage to summer grazing pastures. The floods may have upset the entire watershed in the Ruby Mountains."

"That bad, huh?"

Nate nodded. "We had an avalanche in Lamoille Canyon that pushed one of the restrooms in the campground almost four hundred feet away. It ended up on the other side of the valley. We've never yet found some of the signs. Probably buried under new mountains of dirt. We've got a lot of work to do."

Hank's expectant smile faded, replaced by a bland frown of acceptance. "Well, it was worth asking. I know you're busy with the Forest Service. It's a good career with benefits. It'll take care of you in your old age. Not like me with a ranch I'm too feeble to keep up anymore and no strong sons to work it with me."

Nate hated the thought of this ailing man out here all alone once Lily left, slowly watching his ranch fade into ruin while he couldn't lift a hand to stop it. But what Hank was asking would take a big commitment from Nate. It'd mean he'd be here at Emerald Ranch almost every evening and weekend. With him around all the time, Lily'd only come to resent him more.

A long, swelling silence followed.

"Well, I best be getting back to work. Thanks for lunch," Nate finally said.

Hank didn't look up as he stood. "Yeah, thanks for stopping by, Nate. You're welcome here anytime. Anytime at all."

Nate doubted that, at least where Lily was concerned. But he decided not to mention her obvious dislike for him.

Hank walked Nate outside to his truck and said farewell. As Nate pulled away from the house, he wished he could help this man and his daughter, but he didn't see how. Nate's days were filled with long hours performing watershed studies, building Bailey bridges, completing reports and dealing with irate grazing permittees. He'd already spent too much time dawdling over Lily and her father. And yet he didn't regret it one bit. He cared about the Hansens, which wasn't good because caring made his heart vulnerable.

But what if he delegated a few projects to his assistants? If he asked, they'd take on a bit more work for him. Then he might be able to cut back a few evenings and Saturdays so he'd have time to work here at Emerald Ranch. His range assistant was pretty busy working with the local grazing permittees, but his fire assistant could help more. Maybe Nate could free up some time so he could help Hank.

Nah! What was he thinking? He was a forest ranger, not a rodeo man or a horse trainer anymore. Besides, Lily hated him. Nate didn't want to work where he wasn't wanted. If Hank were smart, he'd sell Emerald Ranch and retire to a comfortable house in town where he could finish out his life in ease and comfort.

Such a shame. Nate gazed at the empty fields where tall hay and alfalfa waved in the wind, waiting to be bailed into hay. And the barn sure could use a fresh coat of paint. With hard work, this could be a lucrative ranch again. It wouldn't take much to get it in pristine condition. Just a few year's hard work and a handful of foals fathered by Peg and they'd be able to sell the horses for a high price. Then they could hire a couple of workhands.

It wasn't Nate's business. He should stop worrying about the Hansens and their ranch. And he definitely should stop stressing over Lily and her child.

He caught a movement at one of the windows and saw Lily watching him from inside her bedroom. He waved, but she drew back, letting the lace curtains drop across the glass pane. From this distance, Nate wasn't sure, but he thought her eyes looked red, as if she'd been crying. And that bothered him most of all.

She wasn't his woman.

Shaking his head, Nate focused on the dirt road as he

pressed the accelerator. He wished he could get Lily off his mind. Her father's predicament pulled at his heartstrings, reminding him of his mom. He must be the oddest of men. Because rather than drive him away, Lily's pregnancy, her estranged relationship with her father and the distrust Nate saw in her eyes every time she looked at him, only made Nate want to draw nearer to her.

Maybe it was good he'd remained a bachelor for so long. Getting tangled up with a gal like Lily would do nothing but complicate his life. And he didn't want complications. No sirree. Not ever.

Chapter Eight

The day before her prenatal exam, Lily rose early. Dressed in faded blue jeans and a ratty T-shirt, she pulled her long hair back in a ponytail before working in the garden. Just yesterday, Myra Stokely had brought her a box filled with soft receiving blankets, baby quilts and little clothes. Myra had wanted to throw a baby shower for her, until Lily confided that she might not keep the baby. Rather than criticize her, Myra had hugged Lily and offered her support in whatever she decided.

Dad had left the house early, going outside to feed the livestock. His persistent cough sounded no better since he'd taken his medicine. Lily helped him pitch hay for a while, then went inside to escape his brusque temper. Tomorrow, she'd go into town for her doctor's appointment, to buy groceries and a couple of six packs of tomato plants. She'd borrow Dad's truck and hope he wouldn't accompany her. She planned to ask Dr. Kenner some blunt questions about Dad's health. Spying on her own father didn't sit well with Lily, but she had to know if he was okay.

That afternoon, as she dusted the living room, she noticed a stack of opened mail sitting on top of the TV set. Scooping it up, she tidied the pile and prepared to set it over on the desk when bright red lettering and the words *past due* scrawled across the top caught her eye.

Picking up the envelope, she studied the return address from Bill Stokely. Unable to resist the urge, Lily slid her finger across the open seam and lifted the flap of the envelope. A handwritten invoice for two hundred bales of grass hay and twenty bags of grain purchased in January spilled out onto her palm. Again, the words *past due* were written in large letters at the top.

A quizzical sensation settled in Lily's stomach. Myra hadn't mentioned the invoice when she'd brought the baby blankets. Lily couldn't help wondering why Dad hadn't paid the bill. Maybe he was disputing the charges. Or was there some other reason Dad had let the account grow delinquent? Regardless, the matter needed to be settled. Feuding with their good friends over a feed bill was not smart. Especially once they ran out of hay. Soon enough, they'd need to buy more feed for the horses. And Bill Stokely wouldn't provide the hay unless Dad paid off the delinquent invoice.

Lily placed the invoice aside on the desk, deciding to speak with Dad about this later. By early afternoon, she'd sorted piles of dirty laundry, started the washing machine, cleaned the single bathroom she shared with Dad, shaken out the rugs and swept the floors in preparation of a good mopping. The phone rang and she didn't hesitate to answer it.

"Hello?"

"Is Henry Hansen available?"

"No, he's not here right now. May I take a message for him?"

"Is this his wife?"

"No, I'm his daughter." She reached for a notepad and pen on the cluttered desk.

"Would you ask him to return my call?"

"Sure." She waited for the information.

"This is Sheldon with Honor One Credit Company. We've left numerous messages for Mr. Hansen, but he's never returned our calls."

A dark foreboding swept Lily, making her hands shake. "What's this about?"

"He's seven months past due on his payments and we'll have to refer him to a collection agency if he doesn't make some arrangements to bring his account current."

Lily froze. "Is this for a credit card?"

"Yes, and he has a rather large balance due."

"I…I'll give him the message."

Embarrassment flooded her face. Even as hard up for cash as she was right now, she'd still found a way to pay her last electric bill before leaving to come home to Emerald Ranch. She wrote down the phone number before hanging up the phone. Confusion filled her mind. She didn't understand what was going on. All her life, Dad had raised her to be honest and pay her debts. To forgo any wants before taking care of the needs. To finish the work before indulging in play. Duty, diligence and obedience always took precedence over everything else. But something wasn't right here. Dad would never ignore the payment of his bills. Unless he just didn't have the money. In which case he'd sell something to pay his debts.

Such as livestock.

Understanding washed over Lily like a flood of icy water. Dad was broke. He must be. That's why he had no cattle on the place. Because he'd sold them to pay his bills. But raising cattle and horses would give him more money.

Unless he didn't have the strength to do the work anymore.

The thought blistered her mind. Dad was ailing. She could discern that with her own eyes. But she didn't know how serious his condition was or how permanent.

Why wouldn't he confide in her? This was her father, not a stranger on the street. Since her return home, too many things didn't add up. Dad's pale face and cough. The ragged state of the ranch. The overdue bills.

Hurrying to finish her chores, she then prepared supper. A pot of homemade stew. Simple and easy. It could simmer on the stove until dinnertime. While they ate, she would calmly ask Dad some questions. She wouldn't let him evade her this time. She'd insist on knowing the truth.

The sound of Beans barking outside brought her attention to the front of the house. Peering out the living room window, Lily saw a blue sedan parked in the wide driveway. Beans stood at the side of the car, barking his head off. A woman got out of the car, carrying a plate wrapped with plastic and a large paper bag. She didn't seem perturbed by the dog, but merely told the animal to knock it off. Beans kept right on barking.

Clara Richens. Formerly Clara Hawkins. One of the nurses from the clinic in town and Lily's best childhood friend.

Lily groaned out loud. The last thing she wanted was for her old friend to come snooping around. Because Clara had been at the clinic when Nate brought her in, the woman already knew Lily was pregnant. As kids, they'd confided all their hopes and dreams to one another. Except for graduating from high school, Lily had yet to meet even one of her goals. The last thing she wanted was to admit her failures to her old friend.

A short knock sounded on the front door. Beans barked louder.

Lily cast a quick glance in the mirror before answering the door. She groaned again, threading her fingers through her tangled hair. As suspected, she looked grungy and haggard. A pregnant woman who'd been feeding livestock and cleaning house all day. Definitely not the way she'd like to greet a guest.

Taking a deep breath, Lily opened the door wide.

"Hi, Clara. What brings you out to the ranch?" She forced herself to smile.

Clara lifted the plate and Lily gazed at a dozen perfectly decorated cupcakes with pink icing and little purple flowers on top. "I thought you deserved a homecoming welcome. I also figured you could use some of my old maternity clothes because you lost all your stuff in the flash flood."

Lily took the plate and paper bag, her mouth watering to bite into one of the cupcakes this very moment. It seemed she had a constant craving for anything sweet. And she really could use the outfits.

"That's so nice of you. I'll be sure to return the clothes once the baby comes."

Clara waved a hand in the air and laughed. "No hurry. It'll be a while before I have a third baby."

"Would you like to come in for a while?" Lily asked, though she hoped Clara declined. Making light conversation when she had so much to do was the last thing Lily wanted right now.

"I'd love to. I actually have a question I want to ask you." Clara brushed past her and stepped into the tidy living room.

Gritting her teeth to hold back an exasperated sigh, Lily closed the door. Without being invited, Clara sat on the worn sofa and looked around the room. The scent of pine cleaner filled the air. Even though she'd finished most of her work, Lily hadn't yet put away the vacuum or box of cleaning rags.

"Looks like you've been working hard today," Clara remarked.

"Yes." Lily set the bag of clothes on the floor and the cupcakes on the kitchen table, planning to devour one just as soon as Clara left.

Lily returned to the living room, and Clara stood and hugged her tight. "Oh, how I've missed you. I'm so glad you've come home, Flower."

Flower. The nickname Clara had given Lily when they were no more than ten years old. The kind gesture warmed Lily's heart and she hugged Clara back. Maybe her friend hadn't come here to gloat after all.

When Lily sat back in Dad's recliner, Clara resumed her seat on the sofa and leaned forward, resting her elbows on her knees. "How have you been, Lily? I haven't seen you in so long. And you never said goodbye. The last time we saw each other, you'd had a terrible fight with your dad. Then you were gone. He said you'd called a week later to tell him you'd run off with that cowboy you met at the county fair. I've wondered and worried about you all these years, hoping you were all right. Hoping you were getting along okay. Have you been happy?"

Clara was just as blunt as ever. Lily shouldn't be surprised. Back in high school, Lily had been the quiet one while Clara had always been loud and outgoing, saying exactly what was on her mind. Maybe that was why they'd been such great friends. Because they complemented each other so well. But that had been a long, long time ago. Now, Lily didn't trust anyone. Not even herself.

"I...I've been fine. The years have gone by fast. I guess you got married." Lily rested a hand across her stomach, feeling self-conscious. She nodded at the gold wedding band winking at her from Clara's left hand, trying to focus the conversation on Clara instead of herself.

"Yeah, Michael and I have been married almost five years now. We met in college. You don't know him, but he's a real nice man. Maybe you can meet him sometime. We have two kids, a boy and a new baby girl." Clara's eyes glittered with pleasure as she spoke of her family.

Lily nodded and smiled as Clara rambled on, but she heard very little. Deep inside her heart, Lily felt like such a failure compared to Clara's accomplishments. A nurse, wife and mother, Clara seemed to have it all. In contrast, Lily had done nothing with her life except make mistake after mistake.

But no more.

Clara's twinkling gaze rested on Lily. "I've missed you so much. Except for Michael, I've never had a friend like you since high school, Lily."

Lily couldn't help feeling pleased by her friend's words. Yet years of suspicion and guilt kept her from confiding in Clara. She felt too ashamed. No doubt Clara would recoil with shock if Lily told her all the things she'd done in the past.

"Look, I don't mean to pry," Clara said. "I'm certainly not in a position to judge others. You might as well know that Michael and I...we had to get married, Lily. I've been where you are. I just wanted you to know you're not alone."

Lily's mouth dropped open in surprise. Clara's admission brought the burn of tears to Lily's eyes. To actually meet someone who knew what she was going through eased the leaden weight in her chest just a bit. But she guessed that Michael hadn't ever beat up Clara. And he hadn't lied about being married to someone else. He'd loved her and made her his wife. And that's where Lily and Clara differed.

"I...I wish I could say getting pregnant out of wedlock was the only difficult thing I've done in my life." The confession was hard for Lily to make.

Clara shrugged. "Like I said, I'm not about to judge you when I've got so many skeletons in my own closet."

Really? Did Lily dare believe her friend? Maybe she could find companionship and acceptance here in Jasper after all, if only until she had her baby.

"There is life after an unwed pregnancy," Clara said. "Michael and I made a mistake, but then we made it right. I can see you're trying to do the same."

Lily wondered if it was possible to ever make her life right again.

"Your life isn't over, Lily. And neither is your baby's. It's just beginning."

How Lily wished this was true. From where she was sitting, she could hardly believe it, although she wanted to. Very much. "Thanks, Clara. I appreciate your support. More than I can say."

"Good, because I want us to be friends again. Close friends, like we used to be back in high school."

Lily gave an uncertain nod. "I'd like that. Very much."

"To start off with, I'd like to throw you a baby shower."

Lily swallowed a gasp. "No, Clara. Please don't."

"Why not? It's a great way to get the things you'll need for the baby. And you need a fun party, too."

Lily bit her bottom lip. Then, taking a small leap of faith, she explained about her indecision in keeping the baby. "So you can see why I can't let you throw me a baby shower. It would just make my decision more difficult."

Clara nodded, her expression sad. "Yes, I do understand and I respect your wishes. I can't tell you what to do, Lily. But I can say that children are a blessing. Hands full when they're young and hearts full once they're raised."

Lily thought this over for several moments. "I believe you're right. But I may simply be the incubator for someone else's daughter. I know my body has made this sweet little baby, but she may not belong to me. The Lord may want her to go to another family who'll love and raise her as their own."

This thought brought Lily deep, abiding sadness. How could having a child bring her so much misery, yet give so much joy to an adoptive family?

"Have you contacted an adoption agency yet?"

"No." She'd have to do that soon, but she dreaded it.

"I have a request," Clara said. "You remember I wanted to ask you a question. Knowing you, you're going to try to stay hidden out here at Emerald Ranch until the baby's born and I can't let that happen. You're back home now and I think you need to laugh now and then."

Lily couldn't remember the last time she'd really laughed. Happiness seemed such an alien emotion anymore. "What did you have in mind?"

"I'm the co-chair of the Jasper Rodeo Committee and I'd like your help," Clara said.

"What?" Never in a million years would Lily have suspected such a request.

Clara shrugged. "Let's face it, you were always better at barrel racing and cutting than I was. You'd be great on the committee."

"No." Lily was shaking her head even before Clara finished speaking. "I hate rodeo now, Clara. I don't want to get anywhere near it ever again. And I'm in no condition to ride anyway." She rubbed her stomach for emphasis.

The truth was, rodeo brought back too many bad memories of her life up until now. And Tommy, the man she'd thought she loved before he'd betrayed and abused her again and again. Rodeo was like a drug in her blood and she wanted to avoid the addiction. To stay away from the type of men who drove into town with a horse trailer long enough to compete, have a fling and leave again. No promises. No commitments. No real love.

Clara tossed her head before standing. "Phooey. No one's gonna make you ride. We want you to help plan the events. You can do that sitting in a chair with a phone next to you. The next meeting will be on the twentieth at seven o'clock at the town hall. I'll expect you there."

She headed for the door, ignoring Lily's look of frustration. Clara paused, her hand resting on the doorknob as she looked over her shoulder at Lily. "You better be there or I'll come after you, Lily. I've done it before, so you know I will."

Childhood memories flooded Lily's mind of Clara track-

ng her down and dragging her to the school play tryouts.
Drill team and cheerleading tryouts. School fundraisers. Clara
always made Lily go with her. They'd been inseparable.

"All right, I'll come." Lily couldn't help chuckling. Maybe
this could be fun. She didn't need to mingle with the rodeo
bums to plan the events. But a little outside activity might take
her mind off her troubles. And get her away from the friction
she had here at home with Dad.

Clara winked at her and smiled. "Good. And welcome
home."

Without another word, Clara left. Lily sat there for some
time afterward, wondering if she dared miss the meeting.
Knowing Clara, she'd come after her, just as she'd threatened.

"You should go."

Lily turned and found her father standing beside the back
door. His gray eyes narrowed with sincerity and she turned
away. He must have overheard part of her conversation with
Clara.

"I will, but I'm not sure I have the time."

"You have all the time in the world, darlin'."

She stood and walked past him into the kitchen where she
stirred the stew with a wooden spoon. "In my present condition, there may be times when I don't feel up to it."

"Bah! You have no excuses, girl." He washed his hands in
the sink before drying them and reaching for bowls to set the
table.

"Dad, you received a phone call today." She told him
about the creditor and showed him the overdue bill from Bill
Stokely.

"What's going on, Dad?" She kept her voice even and non-
accusatory. She was the last person on earth to judge him.

She'd come home, thinking of herself and the predicament
she'd gotten herself in. Now he needed help. Her help. It was
time she started thinking about him. Perhaps leaving Emer-

ald Ranch wasn't an option. Not if Dad was sick and lacking money to take care of himself.

"Don't worry about it, darlin'. I'll get the money somehow."

"You're broke, aren't you, Dad?"

"I have enough for what we need."

"Not if you can't pay your bills."

He nodded, his ruddy face mottled with shame. Seeing her big, strong, blustering father reduced to penury twisted Lily's heart into a knot of flames. It was tempting to kick him while he was down. To chastise him the way he'd always criticized her. And yet, she couldn't. She could see he was hurting inside. All she wanted was to show him compassion.

He lifted one calloused hand in the air. "I'm not broke, just cash-poor. I still have Peg. But my bank account is pretty tight. I've put it off as long as I can, but I may need to sell the quarterhorses."

"No! You won't get much for greenbroke quarterhorses," she observed.

"I've got the mares, too."

"You don't want to give the mares away. They're your way out of financial duress. Once they foal, you'll be able to train the young horses and sell them for a handsome price, especially with their impressive bloodline. The foals will be worth a lot more if we train them first."

"But I need money now. The only other choice is to sell Peg."

"No! You can't do that, Dad." The words burst from Lily's mouth like an explosion. The thought of selling Peg upset every sensible thought in her head. That stallion could make Emerald Ranch profitable again.

"It takes capital and man power to keep a place afloat. And I'm tapped out. I...I can't work much anymore." He gave a sad smile. "I'm getting old, darlin'."

As she gazed into his hazel eyes, her heart melted. He's

asked for her help. How could she refuse him? "Don't worry about it right now, Daddy. We've got a little more time to work things out. First, let's have our dinner. Tomorrow I'm gonna need to borrow the truck. I've got to drive into town for my doctor's appointment and to pick up a few groceries."

"Fine. We have enough money for food. You get whatever you need for the baby, too."

"Not until I've decided to keep her."

"You don't think we can love her enough?"

"That's not it at all, Dad. I just don't want to ruin her life because I selfishly decided to keep her."

"I don't know how to not get excited for my first grand-child. I haven't had much to be happy about in years. I've always looked forward to having grandbabies, and now you're telling me I can't love this little one. It doesn't work that way for me, darlin'."

"I'm sorry things haven't worked out the way either of us planned, Dad."

"Yeah, me, too. You get the groceries we need. I pay my account at Manson's Grocery Store in advance, so you just have them deduct the bill from that."

A leaden weight filled the empty place where Lily's heart sat inside her chest. Paying your account in advance meant he'd had financial trouble in the past and could no longer get credit at the grocery store. His voice sounded light enough, but she detected no earnestness in his tone. No sincerity. No joy.

Just resignation.

Well, that was going to change. Lily was determined not to let her father down. Not ever again.

She was going to do something to keep Emerald Ranch afloat. No matter what, she was not about to watch her father lose his ranch.

Chapter Nine

Lily awakened with a jerk. A pounding filled her ears as she opened her eyes and stared into the dark of her bedroom. Moonlight gleamed through her open window. Lying on her back, she pressed a hand to her stomach, feeling the perfect outline of a miniature foot with her fingertips. The foot moved, thumping against her ribs. Lily gasped in surprise.

Beans barked and voices sounded outside the house. Someone was here, hammering on the front door.

"Bill, what on earth is going on?"

Lily heard her father's gruff voice coming from the living room followed by a woman's muffled crying.

Swinging her legs over the side of the bed, Lily stood and reached for her fluffy bathrobe. Pulling it on, she tied it securely over her tummy before tucking her feet into her slippers and padding down the dark hallway.

The overhead light glimmered from the kitchen. Myra Stokely sat shivering on the edge of the couch, the hem of her pink nightgown damp, her straight, short hair sticking up in places. Sobs trembled over her body and fear radiated from her gray eyes. Bill and his son, Rob, stood beside her wearing an odd assortment of blue jeans, boots and undershirts. It looked like they'd all gotten dressed pretty fast.

"And it took us completely off guard." Bill's booming voice vibrated with distress. "We heard a loud noise and when I got out of bed to check it out, I found myself standing in a foot of muddy water. The electricity was out, so I couldn't turn on any lights to see what was happening."

Without a word, Lily swept an afghan around Myra's shoulders and sat beside the woman on the couch. She rubbed Myra's thin shoulders to help get her warm. Myra gave a cheerless smile and patted Lily's hand in gratitude.

"Thank you, dear." Her voice wobbled.

"Are you okay?" Lily asked.

Myra nodded, her body shuddering as though she were in shock.

"You mean you had a flood?" Dad asked Bill.

"Yeah, a flood. I don't know where the water came from, though. It's too dark to tell yet. I got Myra and Rob out of there as fast as I could. We came here because you're the closest neighbor. We won't be able to tell what happened until daylight."

A bad premonition rested on Lily's heart. She couldn't help remembering Nate's warnings. Had a debris torrent hit the Stokelys' house? Or was this flood caused by faulty plumbing or something else?

"I'll get dressed and find you some dry clothes." Hank headed down the hall toward his bedroom.

Lily braced a hand against the couch and arched her back so she could stand. Her advancing pregnancy had made her balance a bit awkward. "I'll get Myra something warm to wear and then call the volunteer fire department in town."

She did so, then called Nathan Coates at his home. In spite of it being just after three in the morning, he sounded wide awake when he answered the phone. In a few brief sentences, Lily explained what had happened.

"The Stokelys are safe at your house now?" he asked.

"Yes, they're safe."

"Thank goodness. Are you all right, Lil?"

Lil. No one had ever called her that before. He sounded so urgent that she didn't have the heart to chastise him. His constant consideration surprised her. "Yes, both Dad and I are just fine."

"Good. I'll be there in twenty minutes."

True to his word, he arrived eighty-five minutes before the fire volunteers. Lily found the opportunity to get dressed and then prepared a hot breakfast for anyone who wanted it. While the men drove over to see what was going on at the Stokelys' place, she and Myra went to the stable to feed the horses. Myra's pale face and teary eyes told Lily that she was frantic with worry.

"Don't fret, Myra. You're all safe now," she said.

"But our ranch. Our home. I don't know what's happening," Myra cried.

"We'll know soon enough. And you're always welcome here."

"You're such a dear girl. So much like your mother."

The compliment touched Lily like nothing else could. To help take Myra's mind off what was going on, Lily kept up a steady stream of chatter. After a few minutes of pitching hay, Myra took hold of her arm and looked her in the eyes.

"If that ranger tells you that your ranch is in danger, you move, Lily. I love my Bill, but he's one stubborn man. I'm just afraid he should have listened to the ranger when he warned us we might be flooded out. Now we may have lost some of our livestock. And I don't need to tell you a rancher can't afford to lose any animals."

Lily agreed, but just nodded in sympathy. It did no good to kick the Stokelys while they were down or reiterate what Myra already knew. They should have moved to higher ground.

"From what Bill said, your house is still standing. You may need to replace some flooring, but your ranch is still there."

"Yes, you're right. And we're alive. We have a lot to be grateful for." Myra blinked and bowed her head, as if thanking God for this small concession.

Lily also carried a prayer in her heart. For the safety of their men and Emerald Ranch.

By midmorning, Dad, Bill and Rob returned. Myra fell into her husband's arms, but she didn't cry while he told her what had happened in the night.

"It was a flood, all right. Tons of trees, boulders and mud came down the mountain. It hit that stand of aspens bordering the ranch. If not for the trees, the debris would have come clean through and taken out our house. Looks like part of the mountain just gave way in a mudslide."

"But the ranger said it was a debris torrent, not a mudslide. They're a bit different," Rob said.

Bill's mouth tightened. "It was a mudslide. I've seen enough to know."

Stubborn to the end.

"We're lucky our house doesn't sit that close to the mountain," Dad said.

Lily silently agreed, but they could still be susceptible to a debris torrent. Nate had been right and she couldn't help asking about him. "Did he go back to town?"

"No, he's still at the Stokelys' place, helping the firemen clear away the mud," Dad said.

Really? Lily couldn't believe this. Nate was the forest ranger, not a fireman. Although Bill had chosen not to take Nate's advice, the ranger hadn't gotten angry and stomped off in a huff. Instead, he'd pitched in to help clean up the mess. What kind of man would do that?

A good one.

The thought filled Lily's mind with misgivings. In spite of

her harsh judgments, Nate was proving to be an exception. Maybe he wasn't like all the other selfish men Lily had fallen for in the past. But that still didn't mean she wanted to get close to Nate.

The night of the rodeo committee meeting came much too quickly for Lily's peace of mind. The past days had been a whirlwind of work. Cleaning stalls. Feeding horses. Disking the fields to plant hay with Dad. Fretting over bills they couldn't pay. Helping Myra Stokely clean the floors of her house enough so they could live there until new carpet could be ordered.

Bill had called in the help of the local ranchers to clear the muck off his front lawn and out of his house. They'd all pitched in, knowing it could easily happen to them one day. It'd been a dirty, pitiful task. Poor Myra.

Even when riding the tractor, Lily was careful not to move too fast or lift too hard and strain her body. But as her condition advanced, the work became fatiguing. Every day, Lily needed a nap, but there just didn't seem to be enough time for such a luxury.

Even though she hadn't let any tears fall, Lily had been feeling weepy all day. Her hormones must be wreaking havoc on her emotions. But that wasn't all. Myra Stokely had dropped by midmorning with a gift of little knitted booties and a pink afghan that felt soft as the down on a baby chick. Holding the miniature booties on her open palm, Lily imagined bathing, dressing and cuddling her child in the near future. Gifts like this made it harder to think about giving up her baby.

While she changed into one of the clean maternity blouses Clara had brought her, Lily couldn't help thinking about Dad. He seemed happy to have her home, but the tension between them hadn't eased. Whenever the subject of the baby came up, they ended with an argument. Only in work did they find a comfortable camaraderie. Because the Stokelys needed her help, she'd canceled her doctor's visit. Tomorrow, no matter what, she was going to see the doctor.

She stepped into the living room and found Dad in his ragged old recliner, the footrest up, his body stretched out in sleep. His breathing sounded labored and shallow. She didn't like it. Not one bit.

The TV was on, the evening news discussing the hot, rainy weather across the state. Dad snorted and woke himself up. He blinked his eyes at her and smiled.

"You on your way into town for the rodeo meeting?" he asked.

"Yes. I shouldn't be gone long."

He kicked back the footrest and started to stand, but she waved him back. "Don't get up, Dad."

He nodded at the desk. "There are my keys. Have fun."

She doubted it, but gave him a peck on the forehead. "Thanks, Daddy. See you later."

Evening sunlight showed the way along the road leading into town. When she crossed the Bailey bridge, she stared straight ahead and tried to pretend she wasn't crossing the swollen river.

By the time she arrived at the town hall, she was late. Mainly because she'd sat out in the parking lot, arguing with herself about going in. She didn't want to be here. In fact, she wished she could hole up in her bedroom for the rest of her life. But she knew that wasn't healthy, for her or the baby. She just didn't want to deal with anyone's censure. Clara had been kind, but other people might not be. And she was so mentally and spiritually tired. If God couldn't forgive her, she wished she could forgive herself.

As she got out of the truck, she caught the pungent scent of freshly cut grass. The sprinkler swished back and forth across the green lawn. The setting sun glistened on the damp pavement. Inside the red brick building, she followed the sounds of voices to a room where numerous people sat around a large conference table. Clara stood at the front, gesturing to a diagram on the wall of rodeo events. She paused in her dialogue and smiled at Lily. Heads turned and Lily felt as though everyone were staring at her. The only available seat was halfway around the room. She made a beeline for it and slid into her seat before taking out a notepad from her purse.

Clara kept talking, as though nothing had happened. Taking a deep, settling breath, Lily pretended her pulse wasn't racing. Under the pretense of listening, she took a moment to survey the room, self-consciously folding her hands across her abdomen. She didn't recognize several people. Some included fellow ranchers her father's age. An older-looking Clarence Ogilvie, who had always owned the feed and grain store in town. Ted Mortensen, who was two years ahead of Lily in school and had been voted the most likely to become a rodeo bum.

Scratch getting tied up with him in the future.

Next came Sherry Larston, who Lily had soundly beaten at barrel racing every single year of the rodeo when they were growing up. Sherry stared with open disdain at Lily's stomach. No doubt she knew about Lily's fall from grace and Lily quickly moved her gaze to the next person...and froze.

Nate Coates.

He sat directly opposite from her, his gentle eyes boring into hers like a high-speed drill. At first sight of him, her heart gave an odd little jerk. She swallowed hard, wondering why this man's presence unsettled her so much. Why she felt annoyed and yet calm all at once.

He seemed so confident in his own knowledge and abilities. So in control all the time. It didn't help when he winked at her before turning his gaze back to Clara.

Lily blinked and looked away. This man seemed to turn up everywhere she went. Well, he had a right to be here, the same as her. She'd just focus on the meeting, get her assignment and go home.

"We no longer have anyone to chair our Ushers' Committee," Clara was saying. "Would anyone be willing to—?"

Lily shot her hand up. "I'll do it."

How hard could it be? She wouldn't have to mingle with rodeo jocks and she could probably do most of her job from home.

Clara's mouth widened with approval. "Okay, you got it. Meet with me for a few minutes after the meeting and I'll give you some information on what needs to be done."

Lily jotted pertinent notes, focusing on dates and the names of chairs serving on other committees who she might need to contact in the future. Twice, she had to get up in the middle of the meeting to go to the ladies' room. No one seemed to notice except Nate. He arched one eyebrow as she moved silently to the door, and then again when she returned. Didn't he know it was rude to stare? The second time he did this, she tossed him a hard-eyed glare. To which he merely sat back, folded his arms, crossed his legs and focused on Clara. As if he hadn't a care in the world.

If she hadn't been feeling so out-of-place, she might have laughed at the situation. But as it was, she wanted to cry instead. Baby emotions were taking their toll on her and she wanted out of this place right now. Stupidity must be the reason she'd agreed to do this for Clara. And a longing to belong. But as she glanced at Nate and found his brooding gaze resting on her big tummy, she decided staying home at the ranch would be the best place for her right now.

The moment the rodeo meeting ended, Lily bolted for the front of the room to speak with Clara. Nate hung back, chatting with Kyle Roderick about security issues, hoping to speak with Lily before he went home to his lonely house. He wanted to find out how she and Hank were getting along at Emerald Ranch.

Clara hugged Lily and Nate barely caught Clara's whispered encouragement. "I'm so glad you came, Lily. My maternity clothes look good on you."

"Thanks. If not for the clothes you loaned me, I might embarrass myself. They fit me much better than the tight old T-shirts I used to wear in high school."

"Good. Remember how we always planned to lend each other maternity and baby clothes once we got married?"

Lily nodded, her eyes filled with melancholy.

Clara chuckled. "When we started the meeting and you weren't here, I feared I might have to pay another visit to you tomorrow. You'll be perfect for the Ushers' Committee."

"I hope you're right." A doubtful expression drew Lily's delicate brows together.

Clara handed her a large binder and some files. "Stop worrying. Everything you need is right in here. Just contact the people who served as ushers last year and ask them to do it again. They always help out because they get free tickets to the rodeo. You can use this building to meet with your people. Just let me know when and I can reserve the room for you."

"Okay, thanks."

"You'll be working closely with Nate Coates," Clara continued. "He's in charge of security. You'll want to coordinate your activities with him."

A derisive laugh slid from Lily's throat. "Of course. Just my luck."

Nate heard the annoyance in her voice and wished she didn't dislike him so much. Her gaze met his and her chin lifted in challenge.

"If you have any questions, just give me a call. Anytime,

night or day. I'll come running if you ever need me." Clara stepped away to speak with someone else and Lily moved toward the door.

Ted Mortensen intercepted her.

"Hi, Lily! It's been a long time." Ted leaned close, his eyes all over her as she backed up against the wall.

"Hello, Ted." She squared her shoulders and lifted her arms slightly, which were filled with the files Clara had just given her. The documents blocked her round stomach from view.

"Where have you been these past years?" Ted asked.

"Oh, here and there."

A flash of panic filled her eyes and she stared at Ted's shoulders, looking tense as a wound top. Nate didn't think before taking a step toward her.

Ted leaned into her and she cringed. "Maybe we could get together sometime. You free tomorrow night?"

"Sorry, Ted. She's already got plans." Nate tugged on Ted's arm to pull him away from Lily.

Ted pivoted on his boot heels, his mouth open in surprise. At the same time, Lily heaved a sigh of relief and moved to Nate's side.

Ted's forehead crinkled with repugnance and his gaze swerved to Lily. He jerked a thumb toward Nate, his voice filled with revulsion. "Ain't the ranger a bit old for you, Lily?"

Her jaw hardened. "It's none of your business."

She set the files on the table before smoothing a hand over her rounding stomach. Ted's gaze lowered and his eyes widened. The big fool.

Without another word, Lily picked up the files and headed toward the door, tossing an icy glare over her shoulder at the two men.

Determined to work with Lily for the good of the rodeo, Nate hurried to catch up. Ted stared after them, shaking his head in disgust.

"Hey, Lily, looks like you and I will be working together," Nate called.

"Yeah. I didn't know you'd be here, too."

What did that mean? Would she have refused to serve on the committee if she'd known he would be working with her?

She kept walking, her long hair swaying with her brisk stride.

"Maybe we could meet to go over a few things before we pull our committees together." He thought the suggestion was a good idea. He longed to show her that he meant no harm.

"Maybe," she responded, her gaze darting to the door as if she longed to escape.

"When would be a good time for you?"

She jerked a shoulder. "Um, I'd have to check with Dad. Next week sometime."

"Okay, how about if I give you a call tomorrow and we can set something up?" He smiled, hoping to alleviate her fears.

"Yeah, but just remember, it's business only. Nothing more."

He opened the door for her and she stepped past him out into the parking lot. He stood there watching her go. She waddled slightly and he found the sight endearing. It made him feel even more protective of her.

Standing beside her father's truck, she dug through her purse to find her keys. When she jerked open the door and got inside, she tossed him a frosty glare. She had spunk, that was for sure.

Deciding to ignore her bad humor, he waved and smiled. He wasn't interested in a romantic relationship with any woman. So why had Ted made him so angry? Frankly, Nate had his career to keep him busy. He didn't want someone to tie him down, and hadn't found someone who made his heart feel all warm and fuzzy every time he saw her.

Until now.

Just his luck. The first woman to make Nate think of raising a family of his own seemed to hate his guts.

Chapter Ten

Lily tightened her fingers around the steering wheel and stared out the windshield of her father's rusty old truck. Sitting in the parking lot of the Forest Service office in town, she gazed at the white frame building. Two yellow daffodils bloomed in a planter box beside the front door. The urge to turn on the ignition and drive away almost overwhelmed her, but she fought it off. She had to do this. She had no other choice.

She hadn't made a conscious decision to drive here. But she had. On autopilot. Half-dazed by the news Dr. Kenner had given her twenty minutes earlier following her prenatal appointment.

Hypertensive heart disease and a serious case of emphysema. That's what Dad had. Doc Kenner hadn't given her details, but he'd told her enough to understand her father's ailment was serious. Doc Kenner figured Lily should know because she was living at the ranch again.

"Maybe you can do something about his eating habits," the doctor had suggested.

Lily thought about the bacon sandwiches they'd eaten for lunch several days ago and she hardened her jaw. That was going to change first thing. Thank goodness Dad had given up smoking the day he found out about his condition. A disease that caused fatigue, shortness of breath and a persistent cough.

And death. Unless taken seriously and dealt with accordingly.

Lily's entire body trembled when she thought of losing her father. She'd taken him for granted all her life. Even during the years she'd been gone, he'd been here in the back of her mind. She'd thought he'd always be here. Waiting.

Now Dad was sick. As her pregnancy continued to advance, Lily wouldn't be able to feed and care for the horses.

Not without help.

Gripping the handle, she opened the door and stepped out of the truck. She still needed to buy groceries before returning home. Dad would be furious if he knew she'd talked to Doc Kenner. But she was furious he hadn't told her the truth.

Dad was dying. If he took good care of himself, he could undo some of the damage to his heart. But not his lungs. If he didn't change his habits, he'd die.

She couldn't think about that. It was too upsetting. Too painful. Instead, she'd decided to take steps to ensure Dad lived.

She'd better make this visit to the forest ranger short and sweet. Eating crow wasn't going to taste good, but neither would bankruptcy and losing Dad. Once more, she needed Nate's help. And after the way she'd treated him, she wouldn't be surprised if he showed her the door with the pointed tip of his leather cowboy boots.

Walking up the graveled path, she forced herself to breathe evenly. Her steps slowed as she reached the front double glass doors and she paused. She couldn't deny she liked Nate. Very much. And that was a big part of the problem. Liking him didn't mean she trusted him. Or any man, for that matter.

Asking Nate for help went against every grain of common sense she still had in her body.

But she'd sacrifice her pride to help her father.

Opening the front door, she stepped into a tidy reception room that smelled of coffee and pine needles. An older woman with short, graying hair sat behind a high desk and smiled pleasantly at her.

"May I help you?"

"Yes, um, I'm here to see the ranger."

"Do you have an appointment with Mr. Coates?" The woman eyed Lily from head to toe, smiling at her baby tummy.

Lily shook her head, feeling awkward in her worn maternity jeans, scuffed cowboy boots and pregnancy blouse. She should have changed into clean clothes before coming into town, but she'd been in such a hurry. Too much work to do back at the ranch. "I'm afraid not. If he's not here, I can come back later."

Lily almost bolted for the door, but the receptionist stopped her. "What's your name and I'll tell him you're here?"

"Oh! Um, Lily Hansen." She whirled back around, feeling dizzy and unsure of what she was about to do. What if Nate told her no?

"Just one moment." The woman stood and disappeared down a long hallway.

Lily's heart pounded and she took several steps toward the outside door. She didn't want to do this.

Reaching out her hand, she clutched the door railing like a lifeline. Released it. Gripped it again, pushed against it and...

"Lil!"

She turned. Nate stood beside the reception desk wearing his Forest Service uniform. He looked just as she remembered him. Tall, handsome and confident.

"This is a pleasant surprise." He stepped toward her, his right hand extended.

Lifting her head, Lily gazed into his startling brown eyes as she shook his hand. His long, warm fingers engulfed hers, the feel of his calloused palm sending shock waves up her arm. His silky voice soaked into every fiber of her being and her senses of him as a man roared into awareness.

Again, an odd familiarity swept her. Like a downy soft blanket from her childhood. She couldn't remember the color of the blanket or where she'd gotten it, but she knew she liked being wrapped up inside of it. Cuddled in its folds, she could pretend she was warm and safe. That's exactly how Nate made her feel. But she knew the feeling was an illusion. It wasn't real or lasting.

She shook her head, trying to clear her odd thoughts. "Hi, Nate. Do you have a minute to speak with me privately?"

"Sure! Come into my office."

He turned and let her precede him down a long hall. The clicking sounds of someone typing on a keyboard and business chatter in one of the offices filtered through the air.

Now what? She wasn't sure how to broach what was on her mind. Sharing her concerns and failings with this seemingly kind man wouldn't come easy, but desperation did crazy things to people. Needing this man's help rubbed her nerves raw. She prayed, silently inside her heart, that Nate would find it within himself to agree to her proposition.

Inside his comfy office, he pointed at a leather chair, his gaze lowering briefly to her tummy. "Have a seat. Can I get you something to drink?"

She shook her head. As she sat, she looked around, gaining insight into this man from the paintings of mule deer, beautiful forest panoramas and a grizzly bear hanging on the walls. A woman's picture sat on his desk in a burnished frame and Lily wondered who the lady was. The subject wore outdated clothes and looked too old to be a sweetheart of Nate. His mother, perhaps?

He sat on a corner of his cluttered desk. One long leg dangled over the side as he crossed his arms, looking at her with eagle-sharp eyes. "So what can I do for you, Lil?"

The way he said her name seemed odd, but she kind of liked it.

Here it was. No more stalling.

"I...I've thought things over and want to ask if you might reconsider working evenings and weekends out at the ranch." She watched Nate closely, to read his expression. Searching for any sign that he might refuse.

He tilted his head, his brows drawing together in a quizzical frown. "I thought you were planning to leave as soon as you had your baby. Why this change of heart?"

She hadn't planned to offer an explanation and decided honesty would work best. She'd promised God no more lies. "Let's just say I'm caught between a rock and a hard case."

He laughed. "I take it Hank is the hard case?"

She nodded. "Dad told me you refused to help out and I figured I might be the reason. I haven't been very nice to you, considering you saved my life. So I thought if I asked you nicely, then you might agree."

His expressive eyes narrowed. As if he could see right through to her spine and discover every one of her flaws. "You don't have any other reason for asking me?"

A surge of heat blazed up the back of her neck. He sure wasn't making this easy for her.

"Frankly, I just came from Dr. Kenner's office." Her voice wobbled as she spoke and she coughed to clear her throat.

"Is that right?" His mouth tightened just a bit.

"Yes, and he told me that Dad's been feeling rather poorly for some time now. Stress and heavy work could make his condition worse."

No reaction from Nate.

"So, I...I thought things over and wanted to ask if you...if you might reconsider working for us."

He rested his palms along the edge of the desk and shook his head, his gaze pinned on her. "I don't understand. You've made it clear you want nothing to do with me."

"Dad trusts you. He says you're the best horse trainer in the area and that's what we need right now."

He snorted. "And you really expect me to agree after everything you've said to me?"

Another layer of guilt settled over her and she looked away. "I'm sorry, Nate. I don't mean to be rude. Truly I'm doing the best I can to hold everything together. I hope you'll forgive me for being so blunt. I want you to work for us at the ranch if you won't push me for more than that."

He didn't move, didn't blink. Just stared at her with those piercing eyes that told her he was thinking this over but he didn't like it. Not at all.

"No, I won't work for you, but I'll work *with* you."

Her heart jerked. "What's the difference?"

"Working for you, I'd receive a regular wage of some kind. Working with you, I get a share in the venture, just like your father proposed. A partnership of sorts."

She eyed him carefully. If he thought he could take advantage of them, he was dead wrong. She'd die before letting this man milk them for all they had invested in their superior horses. "How much of a share do you want?"

His gaze dropped to the hardwood floor while he considered her question. "How about ten percent?"

"That amount is too low. We'll agree to twenty percent, to be paid when we get paid."

A wide grin burst across his face and lit up his expressive eyes. "I'll agree to fifteen percent with one more provision."

"And what's that?"

"I don't break horses. I gentle and train them. Without mental or physical abuse. Which means I take a bit longer, but the end result is unbelievable."

A vision of Tommy gouging the sides of his horses with his sharp spurs while the animal bowed its neck and bucked filled Lily's mind. He'd never trained a horse in his life. Instead, he preferred to break the animal's spirit. And he never really did have a good horse because of it. "That suits me."

"Okay, then. We have an agreement." He nodded with approval.

The next thing she knew, he stood in front of her, reaching out to take her hand in his. He pulled her up while they shook hands to seal the deal. As she gazed up at him, she couldn't help returning his smile. And something soft and warm shifted inside her chest. Like melting butter, only more remarkable because she thought her heart was encased in permafrost.

"I've already delegated some projects to my assistants," he said. "I can be out at the ranch by around six o'clock tonight."

"You mean you'd already planned to work for us?"

"No. Yes. I mean, kind of. I just want to help."

She pulled her hand free and stepped back, feeling rather fuzzy to have gotten her way so easily. And that set off her radar. Because no man ever gave in to her wishes without having ulterior motives. "What's the catch?"

"Catch?" His forehead creased in confusion.

"Let's not pretend. Why would you agree to this so easily unless you have ulterior motives?"

He made a low sound, like deep, rolling thunder. "Some guy really did a number on you, Lily."

Sudden defensiveness struck her and she squared her shoulders. "I don't know what you mean."

"I can tell you have big trust issues."

"That's right," she said. "So don't do anything to betray my trust and we'll get along fine."

"I haven't yet, but you still seem determined not to trust me anyway."

What he said was true. When had she become so cynical? It had happened over the past years. Living a life of sin had made her evasive, guarded and apprehensive. And she didn't want to be that way. Didn't want to be so contemptuous of men in general. "I'll tell you what. You do your job and I'll... I'll offer you my trust. Just don't ever let me down."

"Agreed. But is it really so hard for you to believe a man would want to help you just because he's a nice guy?"

"No. I mean, yes." She released a pensive sigh as a tweak of conscience pricked her heart. "People have to prove themselves to me first. I guess you did that by saving my life." And yet, she still reserved final judgment, not knowing what it would take for her to trust this man. She shook her head, unwilling to back down on this issue. At least not until she trusted her own judgment more.

"Do you ever pray?" The question had slipped out of her mouth before she could think better about it.

"Occasionally. They say prayer is the soul's sincere desire. What have you prayed for recently?"

"That's kind of personal, don't you think?"

"You brought it up, Lil. If you don't mind sharing, I'd honestly like to know."

"I've prayed about a lot of things, including someone to save me from the flash flood. And then you showed up," she said.

"Anything else?"

She lifted one shoulder in a shrug. "Mostly that God will help me do the right things for my baby and keep Dad's health strong."

"And what about love?"

"I don't know what you mean."

He took a step nearer, so close she could see the flecks of gold in his dark brown eyes. "I mean the love of a good man."

"That doesn't exist."

"Oh, I guarantee it exists. But you have to take a chance to let it work."

"No, definitely not." She shook her head hard. "Another man is the last thing I want in my life."

"Sounds pretty lonely to me."

"Well, that's the way I want it from now on." Her voice quivered with emotion and she could have kicked herself.

"And what about your baby's father? You don't think he'll come here looking for you?"

She snorted. "No way."

"Why did he desert you when you needed him the most?"

"Now, that is definitely getting too personal."

"I'm sorry, but I've gotten used to worrying about you. I wish you'd confide in me."

What could she say to that? She couldn't take a leap of faith, but maybe a little hop wouldn't hurt.

"He won't come here. He's too busy explaining our relationship to his wife and children."

Nate's face darkened. "His wife?"

"Yes, I finally figured out why he wouldn't marry me. He was already hitched. His wife called to advise me of the situation. That night when he got home, I confronted him with the truth."

"And?"

She looked away, swamped by memories of hurt and betrayal. "He didn't deny it. He got angry and I...I left."

"You left?"

She nodded. "In an ambulance."

"What? Why?" Outrage choked Nate's low voice.

Something cold and hard tightened inside her chest. A firm

resolve never to be treated that way again. "I don't want to talk about it. Suffice it to say I left town and I'll never go back."

She folded her hands over her round stomach. "I just feel sorry for Tommy's wife."

"Where'd you go after you left?"

"I had a bit of money and rented a studio apartment. I got a job working retail for a while, but between the bad economy and morning sickness, I got laid off. That's when I decided it was time to come home."

"You've suffered a lot, but I admire your inner strength."

"It's not me. It's God. He's helped me make it through everything I've brought upon myself. Through it all, He's never deserted me. Not once. It was hard to come home and admit what I'd done to my father, but it's also felt so freeing. Like I can really start over and make amends for what I've done."

Nate showed a lopsided grin. "Your faith amazes me. You amaze me."

He brushed his fingertips across the back of her hand, but she jerked away. An automatic response she'd learned by being around Tommy's lightning fast reflexes. She'd never known when he might slap her and she'd gotten good at ducking.

Nate didn't push it but just gave her a gentle smile. "Look, Lil, I like your dad. I always have. And I like you, too. A lot. You might as well know it right now, up front."

"You don't even know me."

"You don't have to know everything about a person to like them. I know you're hurting deep inside, but you have faith in the Lord. And I know He can dissolve the pain troubling your heart. I've seen the way you care for your dad. You're a good person."

"Then you can see why I'm not interested in another romance."

"Yeah, and I'm gonna tell you right now that I am. Inter-

ested in you, that is. And I plan to show you that you can
trust me. Not every man is out just for what he can get from
a woman. There're still a few of us who really care and want
something more lasting and special. Before I'm finished training your horses, you're gonna believe in me. And you'll learn
to trust me as much as you trust yourself."

His eyes didn't waver but locked with hers. Her mind
whirled with what he'd said and she didn't know quite how
to respond. No one had ever been so direct with her. She was
used to men playing sneaky little games. Not coming right
out and telling her what he wanted and where he stood.

"That could pose a problem, because I've never trusted
myself, until recently."

"Good. That's all I wanted to hear. I'm glad you've learned
to trust yourself."

"Wait! I thought we agreed to just be friends."

He shrugged one shoulder in a lazy gesture. "That's not
enough for me anymore."

She gave him her frostiest stare. "What do you mean?"

"You're not gonna chase me off, Lil. I'm here to stay. I want
to convince you to go out with me."

Who did he think he was, speaking to her this way? "That
day will never come."

"We'll see."

A happy, giddy sensation spiraled through her stomach. She
wanted to laugh at his candor, but realized the price would be
too high if she gave in to him. "I'm not any woman you would
want, Nate. You'd do well to set your sights elsewhere."

"And what if I've set my sights on you?"

"Then I fear you'll be sadly disappointed."

"You're too hard on yourself, Lily. My best advice is to cut
yourself some slack. Try to enjoy life a little bit more. You
need to laugh. A lot."

"I'm not a horse, Nathan Coates. I have a baby on the way

to think about. I'm not cutting myself or anyone any slack ever again. And my best advice to you is to back off."

A long silence followed with their staring into one another's eyes. She forced herself not to blink. To make him realize she meant what she said and couldn't be budged. Yet he seemed just as determined. She finally broke eye contact and stepped back. Glancing at the door, she wished she could leave. Wished she were anywhere but here.

Hoping to skirt around his tall body, she reached for the doorknob so she could escape.

"I'll have Earl Tippens draw up a contract and send it over to your office for you to sign tomorrow." She spoke over her shoulder.

Earl was an elderly, retired attorney living in town who didn't charge much for his legal services. Lily's father had been using his services for years. They were good friends.

"That sounds fine." Nate smiled and nodded. "Thanks for dropping by. It's been a real pleasure. I'll see you tonight."

She bit her tongue, knowing she'd told him too much and couldn't blame anyone but herself. The thought of seeing him again at the ranch later that evening confused her even more. He filled her with a mixture of fear and anticipation. She longed to believe she could trust this man, but still didn't dare. Maybe over time, her suspicions might diminish.

As she slipped through the door and hurried through the reception room, she refused to look back to see if Nate was still watching her. Only when she pulled out of the parking lot did she allow herself to look in her rearview mirror. She gasped when she saw Nate standing on the front steps of the Forest Service office staring after her, his hands in his pants pockets.

After buying groceries, she headed home. A large detour sign directed her toward the high Bailey bridge across the flooding river.

The truck thumped across the rivets as Lily drove across. The murky waters below rushed across the banks, swamping sagebrush and willows on either side. As she gazed at the swirling water, a sudden frenzy overwhelmed Lily and she couldn't catch her breath. Memories of the flash flood tore through her brain and she cried out. Of its own volition, her foot floored the accelerator and the truck roared across the bridge. A panic attack like none she'd ever experienced made her tremble so hard that she had to pull over and stop the truck on the other side.

Leaning her forehead against the steering wheel, she sat there shaking. Trying to still her troubled heart and mind. Her faith in God sustained her in that moment. But she hadn't planned on everything being this difficult.

She likened her relationship with Nate and her father to the flash flood. Her emotions threatened to swallow her up and bury her beneath a mountain of guilt and fear.

Minutes ticked by while she regained her composure. She patted her baby bump, gazing down as a ripple of movement burst across her stomach. "I know, sweetums. That scared me, too. But we're safe now. Nate had that bridge built so we'd be secure. I prayed for God to send someone to help us, and I guess He sent us Nate."

As she put the truck into gear and started down the dirt road at a slow pace, she wondered what she'd gotten herself into with the handsome forest ranger. Where would this all lead?

Chapter Eleven

As Nate pulled his silver truck into the wide driveway at Emerald Ranch, his gaze rested on Lily. A thread of joy speared his heart and he wondered why seeing this woman made him so happy.

Dressed in blue jeans, cowboy boots and a shirt with the buttons tight across her pregnant tummy, she stood near a horse trailer set up in front of the barn. A haltered cream buckskin mare pranced back and forth in front of the trailer. Wearing leather gloves, Lily held the lead line to the horse in one hand and a stick with a long string attached at the end in the other hand. Now and then, Lily flicked the string at the horse's hind rump. The fluttering string didn't hurt the mare, but it caused her to move her feet.

Parking his truck, Nate got out and walked over to the horse trailer. He gazed at Lily's distended stomach and widened his eyes. He'd never seen a woman so far along in pregnancy train a horse like this. And he wasn't sure he liked Lily being so close to horse hooves. If the animal reared, Lily could be knocked down and seriously hurt.

Most women this far along would be waddling like a duck, but Lily seemed energetic and light on her feet. Because he realized Lily was concentrating on the horse, he didn't speak.

Instead, he sat beside Hank on the loading dock of the barn and watched the show with appreciation for this talented horsewoman.

Hank nodded and spoke low. "Howdy, Nate. Lily's trailer training one of the mares."

"I see that. You sure she's safe?"

"Yeah, Lily knows what she's doing."

Both men watched Lily work. Nate wanted to see if she was as good with horses as Hank claimed. The lead rope was tied to the halter rather than clipped. That would keep it from bonking the horse in the chin if Lily had to jerk on the lead rope to get the horse to back away from her.

Very shrewd.

Holding the lead rope loose in her forward hand, Lily lightly touched the animal's rump from behind to drive the horse forward a step or two. Then she jiggled the rope to cue the mare to back up a couple of steps. Over and over again, she repeated this exercise. Forward, retreat. Forward, retreat. Nate could see the mare relaxing as she became accustomed to the process and began to understand what Lily wanted from her.

The horse blew dust from her nostrils. Lily paused frequently to stroke and reassure the animal, teaching the horse to overcome the flight instinct of a prey animal.

As Nate watched Lily gentle the horse, it occurred to him that he must handle Lily the same way. To earn her trust, he must show her again and again that he meant her no harm. That she could rely on him. And eventually she would come to him on her own terms.

"They say you can tell a lot about a person by the way they treat animals," he told Hank.

"Yep, and my Lily is the best."

There was no betraying the flush of pride on Hank's face.

He loved his daughter. But Nate realized he just didn't know how to show her.

"You ought to tell her that sometimes," Nate suggested.

Hank glanced at him with confusion, then seemed to consider this statement. "Maybe I will."

Nate's appreciation for Lily deepened. She was a good woman. Whatever mistakes she'd made in her past couldn't override the kind person she was deep inside. Caring, generous and giving. He just needed to figure out a way to convince Lily she had all these wonderful qualities. She couldn't run away this time. She had to stay and fight. There was too much to lose if she bolted. Delicate as the flower she was named after, yet strong and determined to face any storm that came her way. With an undying desire to please God and do what was right. A real woman. Nothing superficial or fake. And she stole Nate's breath away every time he saw her.

Soon, Lily drove the horse from behind, getting the mare to put one foot up into the trailer, then back out.

"Step," Lily called in a gentle but firm voice.

Over and over, Lily repeated this process, using the word *step* to cue the horse to what she wanted. One foot in, then out. Finally, she got the horse to put two feet in, then back out. She repeated this many times.

At one point, the horse had two feet in the trailer and impulsively surged forward, as if ready to go in all the way. Acting quickly, Lily backed the horse up instead.

"Step!"

The horse backed up and Nate chuckled. Lily obviously realized the benefit of leaving the horse wanting more. Through this measure, the horse actually wanted to go inside the trailer and would remember that impulse later. Backing the horse up would add to the mare's confidence so she later knew how to get out of the trailer and wouldn't panic once she was inside with walls enclosing her.

After some time, Lily let the mare rest, leading the horse over to greet Nate. "Hi, there. Thanks for coming."

Her flushed face held an iridescent glow. She gave him a smile so bright that he had to blink. No doubt her success with the horse had made her happy.

"You're welcome." He nodded at the mare. "You're doing good work with her."

"Yeah, she's softened right up for you, darlin'," Hank agreed.

With her arm beneath the horse's neck, Lily hugged the mare's head close and rested her left cheek against the horse's cheek. "She's a good girl and learns fast."

"Only because she's got a good trainer," Nate said.

Lily's cheeks brightened and she shifted her weight, seeming embarrassed by the praise.

"Where did you learn your trailer training technique?" Nate asked.

Lily nodded toward Hank and smiled. "Dad taught me years ago. Trailer training Misty is something I can do without riding and worrying about getting bucked off."

Nate hopped down off the docking bay and went to thread his fingers through the mare's dark mane. Her ears pricked forward as he spoke gently to her. "Misty. Your name suits you."

Hank sat up straighter, his mouth widened in a grin. He looked as proud as a cat that had swallowed a canary.

"Dad named her."

Nate studied Lily. She'd pulled her long hair back in a ponytail. Several wispy strands had come loose and framed her face, almost red in the sunshine. He thought he'd never seen anything so beautiful in all his life. "If you learned that technique from your dad, then I think we'll do fine together. I'm anxious to learn a few things myself."

"Well, I'm happy to teach you both." Hank stood and wiped

his tough hands down his pale blue jeans. "But for today, let's just start with feeding the horses. Then I'm gonna go up to the house and fix us some supper and we'll talk about our training schedule. I'm anxious to get the new colts and fillies working."

Hank turned to go inside the stable, but Lily stopped him. "Dad, I know how to feed the horses. I don't want you doing anything but watching Nate and me work."

Lily gazed at her father, hoping he wouldn't fight her on this. Above all else, she wanted to help her father get well. The ranch didn't matter if she lost her father.

Dad pursed his lips and she thought he might argue. A tingle of anxiety swept her.

Dad waved a hand in the air and kept walking. "Okay, so I'll watch."

Lily stared after him, her brow furrowed with concern. She spoke to Nate without looking at him. "You think he'll be okay?"

Nate stood beside her and cleared his throat. "What all did Doc Kenner say he could do?"

"Anything that doesn't require rigorous exercise. Forking hay to horses will get him breathing too hard. He has emphysema and shortness of breath. That makes his heart pump too hard."

"Then I'll do the feeding and make sure he just orders me around."

Lily chuckled. "Believe me, Dad loves ordering people around."

A laugh burst from Nate's throat. "Giving instructions will help him feel useful but shouldn't tire him out."

They walked toward the stable and she couldn't help realizing that she shared a special bond with this man. Maybe it was because he'd saved her life. "I hope you're right."

"You don't want your father to feel useless. Hank isn't the

type of man to just sit around while everyone else is working. Let him do what he can."

Nate's insight pleased her. She paused at the stable, noticing a companionable feeling settled between them.

"I wouldn't let on to your dad that you know about his illness yet," Nate spoke low. "He told me about it and asked me not to tell you. He's afraid you'll worry."

"Well, he's right. You knew and didn't tell me?" She glanced at him, a feeling of outrage flashing through her. "I need to know those kinds of things."

"It wasn't my place. Hank told me in confidence. But now you know, let's try to help him without making him feel like an invalid."

She shook her head but agreed. "You're right. I don't want to hurt Dad. I want to help. And you're the trainer. We're gonna have to work together."

"Wow! It must have taken a lot for you to say that."

"It's the truth. I might as well get used to it." She hoped saying it out loud would help her adjust to Nate being around the ranch all the time.

"How are you feeling?" he asked.

She pressed a hand to the side of her tummy. "Fat and tired, with a raging case of heartburn."

He chuckled. "Why don't you go inside and take a nap? I can take care of this work while you rest."

"Maybe later."

He frowned but followed her inside the stable. The musty scent of fresh straw and animals filled the air. Dad stood beside Peg's stall, tapping his foot impatiently while he waited for them.

Nate paused and considered the stallion. "I'm guessing Peg weighs about twelve hundred pounds, right?"

Dad nodded. "He's on the bigger side for a quarterhorse."

"Good. He's strong and should have more stamina. That'll

help create strong foals. I'm guessing you're feeding him about twenty-four pounds of feed a day?"

Lily stood back and watched while Nate reached for the pitchfork hanging on the wall and broke off two flakes of hay from the bale sitting nearby. As he did so, he eyed the other bales of hay and then the grain.

Not much feed left.

Lily did some mental calculations. The bales consisted of two ties each and weighed about fifty pounds. For that size of bale, they could get about twenty-five flakes per bale. Within a matter of days, they'd run out of feed.

A feeling of panic tore through Lily. They had no money to buy more, unless…

She'd deal with that issue later tonight. Right now, she wanted to focus on Nate and his judgments for feeding their horses.

"Yep," Hank said. "Peg eats about five flakes of hay per day and about two pounds of grain. I feed him twice per day and give him free choice of water and salt."

Nate tossed the hay to the horse, then looked at the near-empty grain bag. "I'd like to increase his intake of grains slowly over the next couple of weeks so we don't cause any problems in his digestive tract. Now that I'll be working the horses more, they'll need a little more hot feed."

Hot feed gave the horse more energy and consisted of oats, barley, wheat and even corn.

"Okay, I agree. We'll…we'll buy some more grain. Somehow," Hank said.

Nate glanced at Hank, looking quizzical.

"And what about the pregnant mares?" Lily asked hurriedly, hoping to distract Nate. She didn't want him to know about their money troubles. It was too embarrassing. They'd solve their own problems. No need to drag Nate into it.

"I suggest we give the mares their hay, but have you got

some high-protein pellets we can give them, too? It's good for their growing babies."

Hank frowned. "We…we ran out about a week ago, but I'll go into town and get some more Saturday."

Again, Lily's flesh heated with frenzy. What would they use for money? They could barely afford to feed themselves, let alone these expensive animals.

Reaching up, she fingered her mother's engagement ring beneath the cotton fabric of her shirt. The ring might fetch a good price.

She looked up and caught Nate staring at her. Feeling self-conscious, she stepped away and busied herself by sweeping out one of the empty stalls. Out of her peripheral vision, she saw Nate studying the meager supplies of hay and grain stacked neatly along one wall where it would stay dry and free of mold.

Reaching down, he took a handful of hay and rubbed it with his fingers before letting it sift through his hand onto the wooden floor. "Who's supplying your hay?"

"Bill Stokely," Lily said.

"Looks like you're due for another delivery soon. This time, tell Bill to put less alfalfa in it. I'd like to see seventy-five percent Timothy grass and twenty-five percent alfalfa." Nate glanced at Hank for his approval.

"I agree. I already talked to Bill about it the last time he delivered hay for me."

Nate smiled. "And in the morning, give the colts and fillies a little hot feed and I'll work them when I get out here in the afternoon."

Lily breathed a sigh of relief. Even though she'd been raised on a ranch and could ride better than most, she had no idea how to feed quality performance horses. Thank goodness Dad and Nate were here to teach her. She was eager to learn and excited by the prospects. Working with horses always made her happy. Dad knew what to do, but the goal was to turn these chores over to Nate so Dad could cut back on his work-load. The fact that Dad kept nodding his head in agreement told her that Nate knew what he was doing, too. And that gave her the confidence to trust Nate.

Just a little bit.

Lily remained outside with the men for another hour, listening to every word exchanged between Nate and Dad, learning from these two masters. As Nate reached for a pitchfork and tossed hay to the horses, she couldn't get over how natural it felt to have him here at the ranch. Like he was part of the family and had always belonged here.

Inside the house, Lily washed her hands before checking on the roast beef she'd put in the slow cooker earlier that day. After setting the table, she speared the potatoes with a sharp knife to check their doneness. Almost ready.

The men came inside speaking animatedly as they washed up.

"Mmm, dinner smells good. Thanks for inviting me." Nate gave her a broad smile.

"You're welcome." She didn't look at him as she responded.

A warm, yeasty aroma filled the air. Homemade rolls ready to come out of the oven. She reached for a hot pad to cover her hand and caught Nate staring at her. He looked away, his face tinted with a flush.

While she sliced the meat, she kept listening to their conversation, her emotions a riot of unease. On the one hand, she was excited by what they planned to do with their horses. The future spread out before them and she had high hopes. On the other hand, they had some gigantic hurdles to jump across if they were to succeed.

After they sat down together and offered a blessing on the food, Nate scooted his chair in close to the table. "You're sure Nibs wouldn't make a good reining horse?"

"Nah!" Dad said. "He fought me hard on learning to stop. Any horse that fights stopping that much won't do well on the long, sliding stop needed for reining. He'd make a better cutter."

"Okay, but we're gonna need some cattle for that."

Lily paused as she spooned steamed asparagus onto Dad's plate. "How many head?"

"Fifteen to twenty should do the trick," Nate said. "Can you swing that many?"

She hoped so. "I'll find a way."

Dad poked the vegetables with his fork. "What's this?"

Lily glanced at him. "Nutrition. Eat it. It's good for you."

Nate chuckled and took a bite of his own asparagus. "Mmm, tastes good. Nice and tender."

"I walked along the ditch banks this morning and collected it." She remembered doing the same thing with her mother on numerous occasions. Dad had never liked asparagus or anything much besides meat and potatoes, but Lily was determined to make sure he ate a balanced diet from now on.

Dad made a squeamish face before he put a piece into his mouth and chewed. Lily almost laughed out loud. Some kids didn't like eating vegetables, but she hadn't figured on having to fight Dad to get him to eat them.

"Where's the butter?" Dad reached for the bowl of steaming potatoes.

Lily handed him the margarine.

His eyes widened in disgust. "What's this?"

"It's lower in cholesterol."

Dad's mouth dropped open and he rubbed his small paunch. "I didn't think I was fat."

"You're not, Dad. But nutrition is more than just about keeping the weight off. You've got to start eating better, so don't argue about it."

He pursed his lips in that expression that told Lily he wasn't pleased but wouldn't fight her on it. And that's when she knew she'd won. For now. But she was also smart enough to realize he could sneak behind her back and eat bad things when she wasn't looking. So she'd cleaned out the kitchen of high-cholesterol foods, bought a carton of egg whites, lots of fresh vegetables and put a bowl of apples, oranges and bananas out on the counter within easy reach. Once her garden started producing, they'd soon have lots of good foods to eat that wouldn't cost a lot of money.

Looking up, Lily found Nate watching her as he chewed a piece of tender meat. He winked at her and she almost returned his smile.

Almost.

Only one day of working together and already she felt more comfortable around this man than anyone she'd ever met. His confidence and way of handling her father put her at ease and she couldn't explain the relaxed atmosphere in the house. Just yesterday, she and Dad were arguing about almost everything. But with Nate here, they all seemed to unwind and float along business as usual.

After dinner, Nate hopped up and helped clear the table while Dad went into the living room and flipped on the TV to watch the evening news.

"You don't need to do that." Lily took the pile of plates out of Nate's hands and set them in the sink she was filling with hot sudsy water.

"I like to help you."

Reaching for a dish towel, he stood close to dry the dishes. Too close.

Lily stepped to the side and made a pretense of wiping off the table with a damp dishcloth. Gone was the friendly camaraderie they'd shared during dinner. Now she felt nervous and hunted. Funny how when they talked about horses and cows, she didn't feel anxious around him. But when they were alone, she became conscious of him as a very handsome, charming man and that made her jittery.

"Lil, I'm glad we have a moment alone," he said.

"Why's that?" She didn't look at him, but scrubbed the glasses, rinsing them and setting them in the dish drain.

"Do you need some money?"

She bit back a gasp and her head came up fast. Was it that obvious?

"If you need financial help, I have some savings set aside and I'd be happy to invest it—"

"No!" she cried. "We're fine. It's just that Dad's been ailing and hasn't taken care of things like he should have done. Now I'm here, I'll get things going again. We'll buy more grain and I'll speak with Bill about delivering some more hay. I don't need you to protect me all the time, Nate."

She'd die before asking this man for money to feed their livestock. No sirree! She would *not* take a handout of that kind.

Nate's mouth curled in a doubtful expression. "Every woman needs a protector, no matter how independent or strong she is. Wouldn't you like to settle down with a family of your own one day?"

She shook her head. "Happily ever after doesn't happen. Not in real life. Not for me."

"Sure it does, if you let it." He smiled again and she found herself almost believing him.

Almost.

By the time he left the house, it was late. They'd all sat in the living room, watching the local news, which came on at eleven o'clock. Afterward, Lily went to her room while Dad walked Nate out to his truck and said goodbye. In the bathroom, Lily washed her face, brushed her teeth, then literally fell exhausted onto her bed. The soft evening breeze and hum of crickets outside her open window soothed her jangled nerves.

In those quiet moments alone, she felt the little thumps of her baby moving inside of her and rested her hands over the gentle swell of her abdomen. During the business of the day, she'd almost forgotten she was pregnant. Almost forgot what had brought her home to Emerald Ranch.

Sliding to her knees, she folded her arms, closed her eyes and leaned against the bed while she offered a silent prayer to her Heavenly Father. Pouring her heart out to Him, she thanked Him for her many blessings and asked for His help. Somehow, they had to get enough money to buy some cows and feed. She didn't know what to do, but somehow—

Lily paused and lifted her head as she opened her eyes and gazed at the far wall. In the shadows, the moonlight caught the gleam of her mother's large engagement ring resting on top of her dresser. The ring meant so much to Lily. But what she wanted most was to preserve the ranch so future generations would have something more tangible and rewarding to enjoy.

Weighing the value of her mother's diamond ring against the value of the ranch was easy. Lily decided then that she wouldn't mourn her decision. She wouldn't allow herself any regret. Instead, she'd move forward with confidence and resolve. She couldn't allow herself to flinch or shirk her duty. Not when there was so much at stake. And with perfect clarity, she knew what to do.

Chapter Twelve

Saturday morning, Nate arrived early at Emerald Ranch with a load of grain in the back of his truck. When he'd seen how low the Hansens were on feed, he'd decided to take the initiative and buy the grain. They could pay him back later, but the horses needed the oats right now.

Without disturbing anyone inside the house, he backed his truck up to the loading dock of the barn, planning to unload the bags and feed the horses. Beans bounded off the front porch and trotted after Nate, giving a couple of shrill barks. The crisp morning air smelled of alfalfa and rain. Nate glanced at the clouds circling the Ruby Mountains and silently prayed the storm might pass them by. Any more rain, and they could have more serious flooding throughout the valley. Evacuating the ranchers from their homes meant a lot of work and inconvenience if they had to move their livestock. Nate didn't want to have to resort to such tactics, but he'd do it if he thought they were unsafe.

After tugging on a pair of leather work gloves, he hefted one of the fifty-pound bags onto his shoulders and carried it to the barn. Beans panted and loped along beside him. Nate almost dropped the bag when he came face-to-face with Lily.

"Whoa!" He veered to the side so he didn't drop the heavy bag on top of her.

She jumped out of the way, shielding her round stomach with one arm. "Nate! I didn't expect you here so early."

He set the bag down, leaning it against a stall door. "Likewise. You startled me."

"Sorry."

He eyed a wheelbarrow sitting nearby filled with manure and dirty straw. "Have you been mucking out the stalls?"

She nodded, her gloved fingers gripping the handle of a manure rake. Her flushed cheeks testified that she'd been working hard. Tendrils of dark hair framed her face. Before he could stop himself, he reached out and tucked a curl of hair back behind her ear.

She stepped away, her face darkening with disapproval. His gaze dropped to her abdomen. He hated the thought of her working hard when she was pregnant. No doubt she was picking up the pace to ease her father's load.

"You shouldn't lift that wheelbarrow. I'll muck out the stalls from now on," he said.

She crinkled her nose. "You're here to train horses, not muck out stalls."

"I can do both chores in half the time it takes you."

"That's ridiculous. I know you're stronger, but I get the job done well enough."

"I know, it's just that I…I don't want you lifting heavy loads. You should get off your feet."

She looped her hands over the top of the fork as she leaned on it and her eyes sparked with fire. "I won't lift too much, but I'd rather you didn't give me orders."

Oh, this wasn't going very well. This was not a woman he could, or should, boss around. She'd been hurt before and didn't like men telling her what to do. He decided on a different tactic. "I don't mean to order you around, Lily. I'm just worried about the baby. Would you please let me clean out the stalls? At least let me move the wheelbarrow once it's full. Really, I don't mind."

Her expression softened. "You can't be here all the time, Nate."

True. And that bothered him. How could he protect her and Hank when he wasn't here? "I'll tell you what. Just shovel the manure into the wheelbarrow and I'll move it in the evenings when I come here after work. It's no big deal. Okay?"

Without waiting for her reply, he took hold of the heavy wheelbarrow and directed it outside to dispose of the contents. When he returned, he found her forking hay to the horses. Prickles of fear dotted his flesh. "I can do that."

He took the pitchfork from her hands. Ignoring her aggravated glare, he broke off several flakes of hay and tossed it to the colts.

"The hay isn't heavy, Nate. And I like feeding the horses."

He didn't look at her but kept on working. "It's not the weight I'm worried about, but how you're moving. You could pull a muscle or strain yourself."

"I don't need a babysitter. I'm not an invalid."

"I know. But I can take care of this for you today."

"What's that?" She tapped the point of her boot against the bag of grain he'd set on the ground.

"Oats. I've got nine more bags out in my truck." He pitched more hay to the horses.

"Who told you to bring it here?"

He paused in his work, bracing the tines of the fork against the ground and cupping a gloved hand over the top of the handle. "I did. I could see you needed the grain, so I thought I'd save you the trip and picked it up at Ogilvie's in town."

She lowered her eyes, looking ashamed for some reason. "How...how did you pay for it?"

"With cash. You can repay me after we sell some of the horses."

"We'll repay you as soon as we can, Nate. I promise."

He flashed her a smile. "I know that, sunshine. No worries."

He felt more than saw her anger at him calling her sunshine. To deal with her reticence, he decided to ignore it.

She reached for an old coffee can with holes drilled through the top for a thin rope handle. Dipping the can into an almost empty bag, she filled the can with rolled oats, then hung the handle on a fish scale to weigh it carefully.

"Who's that for?" he asked.

She brushed her long bangs back from her forehead. "Peg. Surely you're not going to tell me I can't lift a can of grain."

"As long as it doesn't weigh more than ten pounds, it won't bother me."

"Oh, hogwash!" She stepped into Peg's stall. The stallion backed up to let her pass, then came forward when she poured the oats into his feeder.

Nate watched with approval. It was important that they follow a strict feeding regime for each horse, especially now that they were starting to train the colts and fillies. No one knew better than Lily how important the care of these animals was to their financial future. Although Nate had a good, regular paying job with benefits, it was more than important to him that he help the Hansens succeed in their business, too.

Nate stood holding the pitchfork, mesmerized as Lily ran a hand over the stallion's smooth neck. She rubbed the horse's forehead, speaking in hushed tones. Telling the horse how wonderful he was. It took the count of ten for Nate to realize he was staring.

Ducking his head, he finished with the hay. As he passed each stall, he glanced at the inhabitants, thinking about which horse he wanted to work with first. His gaze landed on the three-year-old filly named Toots. Hank had said he'd ridden her with a ring snaffle, but all the horses were green from lack of recent riding.

A chestnut color with a white blaze down her nose and four white feet, Toots backed away from the stall door and faced Nate when he took in her breakfast. Nate liked that. Obviously Hank had taught his horses to back off rather than crowd close when someone entered their stalls. Toots had good ground manners and Nate decided to take her out first.

While the horses ate, Nate surveyed the saddles, bits, supplies and training tools in the tack room. He selected what he wanted and stepped outside. After she'd eaten, he wrapped all four of Toots's legs to give her added support and protect her forelegs from being sliced by her own hooves. Lily assisted him, handing the padding to him, paying close attention to what he did. Then he saddled Toots and put her into a short shank Argentine correction bit. The headsetter included a floating nose. The horse opened her mouth readily to accept the bit, then pressed against it with her tongue and shook her head. She didn't like the strange feel of it in her mouth, but she didn't fight it.

"Why did you adjust the nose strap so loose?" Lily asked.

He secured a small buckle at the side of the horse's nose. "So there won't be any pressure on her nose unless she raises her head up unusually high. The headsetter works off the horse's pull and will help train Toots to keep her head low for cow work."

Taking the reins, he led Toots out to the circular arena. Lily followed and Nate couldn't deny a thrill of excitement at having her near. He glanced at her, enjoying the heightened color in her cheeks. "You sure look pretty today."

She frowned at the compliment.

He couldn't decide if she was always this beautiful or if her pregnancy made her this way. He felt like showing off for her, but realized that wasn't right for a man his age. He could ride well and he knew it, but somehow he realized this woman didn't care about show. What she needed in her life was reliability. A man who would stand beside her and treat her right.

Like always, she'd dressed in blue jeans and boots, her long brown hair pulled back in a ponytail that bounced as she walked. As she stepped up on the bottom rung of the corral, Nate couldn't help wishing she'd leave it long around her face once in a while. His fingers itched to touch the silken softness and he decided to clamp an iron will on his stray thoughts.

She looped her hands over the top rail to hold on and see better at the same time. "What are you going to do with her first?"

After mounting, he loped the horse around the arena, turning her now and then to get a feel for her movements and how she took his hand, feet and leg commands. "First I'm gonna warm her up and see how she feels with me in the saddle. We're just gonna make friends."

"Well, don't let me disturb you. I'll just get the horses some fresh water." She stepped down off the railing and turned.

"It's already done," he called.

She pivoted, looking surprised. "You didn't need to do that."

He smiled and tugged on the brim of his cowboy hat. "My pleasure."

The horse turned and Nate pretended not to see Lily's frown. He expected her to leave, but she stayed while he worked the horse. Knowing she was watching made him feel strangely giddy inside. He wanted to display his skills for her. To prove he could handle this little mare.

Instead, he focused on the horse. No matter what, he could still feel Lily's gaze resting on him. Watching his every move with intense scrutiny.

As he trotted Toots, Nate realized the horse was carrying

her head awfully high. To remedy this, he gave several short
tugs on the reins. She stiffened, fighting him just a bit, so he
added a little more strength to the tugs. Nothing that would
hurt the horse, but just enough to get her to back off from the
pressure. Toots lowered her head and he immediately quit the
succession of light tugs. That was her reward for doing what
he wanted.

"Good girl." He patted her neck to show his pleasure.

Again and again, Nate turned the horse, demanding she
keep her head low. When she turned left or right, he taught
her to pull her nose in tight. This technique would help her in
cattle work when she had to keep a cow from racing back to
the main herd. After all, that was the purpose of a good cutting horse: to never, ever take her eyes off the cow.

Toots quickly learned how to back off the pressure from
Nate's foot commands and his tugs on the reins. The horse
took very little repetition to learn and was soon doing just
what he desired.

For fifteen minutes, he worked with Toots. Then he rode
her over to the fence to chat with Lily and let the horse rest.

"She's getting it," he said. "I've never worked with a horse
that responds so fast."

Lily reached over the fence and rubbed the horse's muzzle.
"Yes, but she's over-rotating a bit when she turns to her right."

"You noticed that, huh? She works her left side pretty well,
but I'm going to have to correct her bad habit on the right side.
She's trying. The mistakes she's making are just honest mistakes. And she's not requiring a lot of instruction to show her
what to do. I wish we had some live cows to practice her on.
She's almost ready for real action."

"I think we'll be able to take care of that problem soon
enough."

"What do you—"

"Hi, Nate." Hank came out of the house wearing a leather vest over his plaid shirt.

"Good morning, Hank. You're looking rested."

Hank chuckled and brushed his graying hair back from his forehead before putting on his crumpled old cowboy hat. "I feel good, too. My daughter fixed me breakfast. Best pancakes I ever ate, although they would have been better with butter and syrup instead of fresh fruit."

"Dad, we talked about this." Lily's voice held a mild scolding quality. No doubt she'd insisted Hank eat what was good for him.

"You hungry?" Hank directed the question to Nate.

"No, I ate before I left home."

"Then go ahead and work. Who do you want to ride next? I can get the horses saddled and ready for you." Hank headed for the stable.

"It doesn't matter at this point. I've got to get to know them all, so bring out the next one you think I should have and we'll talk about their strengths and weaknesses as I see what they need help on."

Within twenty minutes, Nate returned Toots to the stable where he quickly removed the saddle, ensured she was dry and had plenty of water, then fed her a pellet of molasses and compressed hay. The horse gobbled the treat right down, then waved her head as if asking for more.

"You're gonna spoil her."

Nate turned and found Lily close behind him. She laughed at his surprised expression.

"Yeah, but it won't hurt her." He wasn't sure if she was staying close to him today to see if he knew what he was doing, or if she might be starting to like him. He hoped it was the latter.

"Now I know your secret," she said.

He felt a bit out of sorts to be caught giving a treat to the horse. "Try it sometime. Pretty soon, I'll have these horses coming right over to me hoping I'll give them one."

"I'm sure you'll make good friends with every horse on the place."

I hope so, he thought to himself. But what he really wanted was to be friends—good friends—with Lily. Maybe even more than friends. But training horses had taught him the most important lesson of all: patience.

Monday morning, Nate drove down Main Street in town, heading back to the office after meeting with a local rancher. He wanted to complete a watershed study before he drove out to Emerald Ranch to work with the horses that afternoon. As he passed the bank, a flash of red caught his eye. Lily wearing a red sweater came out of the pawn shop, walking fast as she hurried toward her father's truck parked in front. She didn't notice Nate as he drove by. He almost honked the horn to draw her attention but thought better of it. What was she doing in the pawn shop?

He drove two more blocks before he made a U-turn and returned to the store. Parking his truck in the back, he went in through the side entrance.

A little bell tinkled overhead as he opened the door. Carl Jutledge looked up from the front cash register. Window cases lined the room, filled with an odd assortment of jewelry, guns and coins. The air smelled musty, the lighting dim. The whole place had a sleazy feel about it.

"Morning, Ranger. What can I do for you?" Carl grinned, showing yellowed teeth.

"A young woman was just in here." Nate felt a bit uncomfortable inquiring about Lily's personal business, but he had to know what she'd been doing.

"Yeah, so?"

"What did she want?"

Carl's eyes narrowed. "She ain't stolen nothing from you, has she?"

"Of course not. I'd just like to know what she wanted."

Carl showed a worried smile. "The way I see it, it ain't none of your business."

Nate leaned his elbow on the counter, trying to appear casual as he held a twenty-dollar bill between his fingers. "You're right, but I might be able to make it worth your while."

Carl's small eyes wavered between the greenery and Nate's stoic expression. "In that case, she sold me this. It's a rare beauty."

Carl reached for a cloth-lined dish and placed it on the counter. Nate sucked in a slow breath when he saw the size of the sparkling gem displayed in a band of white gold and set off by numerous smaller diamonds. The ring Lily always wore around her neck. Her mother's engagement ring, with a sizable rock that must be worth a tidy sum.

Nate reached to pick it up. "May I?"

"Sure! It's quality, I can tell you."

"How many carats is it?"

"Three and I've confirmed ownership. She had the papers and everything. This diamond's certified. Excellent color and clarity. A real beauty. Worth a small fortune."

Nate gave a low whistle. "Why did she sell the ring to you?"

Carl shrugged. "Said she needed the money. You interested?"

A dark feeling settled in Nate's chest. He'd heard a few things around town about Hank's overdue bills. And from the looks of their hay supply, Nate figured Hank was low on funds. Without asking, Nate realized Lily had pawned her ring so she could help take care of the ranch. But this was her mother's ring. Nate didn't believe Lily would pawn it unless she was utterly desperate for cash.

"Did she say where she got the ring from?" Nate asked.

A totally fake, sad look filled Carl's eyes. Nate knew it was all for show, just to make a sale. "She said it was her momma's ring. Her daddy gave it to her the day her momma died. She hated to part with it, but she figured her mom would understand."

Nate bit back a harsh breath. Lily had sold a priceless heirloom from her mother to keep the ranch safe. Once again, Nate couldn't help admiring Lily. She'd selflessly put aside her own needs to take care of her dad. And all Nate wanted was to make Lily smile.

That evening, Nate was working with one of the colts at Emerald Ranch when Bill Stokely and his son rode up on horses. Herding approximately twenty red and black Angus cows in front of them, the two men waved.

Nate paused, letting the horse beneath him catch his breath for a moment. Lily walked out to greet the Stokelys, then waddled over to the gate, opened it wide and let Bill herd the cows into the pasture. Hank stood in the middle of the yard, his mouth hanging open in surprise. Obviously he hadn't known anything about this.

"Well, I'll be." Nate chuckled beneath his breath. Somehow, Lily must have made a deal with Bill. Pawning her mother's ring wouldn't pay for this many cows. So how had she convinced Bill to give her the beefs?

Nate stepped off the colt and tied the animal to the fence, which would let the horse get used to standing at a tie. Nate then sauntered out into the yard to chat. What he really wanted was information.

"What's going on?" Nate asked Hank.

The two men stood beside the railing of the fence, watching Bill move the cattle farther into the pasture. In one mass, the beefs moved away and then immediately went about grazing on the rich feed.

"I have no idea." Hank leaned his arms against the top rail of the fence.

Lily soon joined them, securing the latch on the gate while Bill ensured the cattle were okay.

"You want to tell me what this is all about?" Hank asked his daughter.

Lily lifted one booted foot up to rest on the bottom rail of the fence. She didn't look at her father, but gazed at the cows. "I made a deal with Bill."

"What kind of deal?"

"He's agreed to let us use his cows for training our cutting horses. In exchange, we'll board the cows here at our place for free."

"What?" The word burst from Hank's mouth like a nuclear explosion.

Lily faced her father, her hands clenched by her sides. Her expression looked tight as a bowstring, her eyes narrowed with ferocity. Nate braced himself for the coming storm. He wanted to intercede, but figured this was between Lily and her father.

"Now, Dad, don't you say one more word about it. We don't have any money to buy cows, but we need them. This pasture is sitting idle. That small herd of cattle isn't going to do any damage to our field. It's a good deal and we need this. So just leave it alone."

Hank blustered like a charging bull, but what could he say? Lily was right. She'd done what she had to do. But from the surprised expression on Hank's face, Nate got the impression that Lily didn't often stand up to her dad with this much conviction. She'd put her foot down and Nate was curious to see if Hank let her have her way.

"And you might as well know," she continued in a gentler

voice, "I've paid off what you owe and bought another load of hay from Bill. He'll be delivering it tomorrow." She glanced at Nate. "I'll pay what we owe you for the oats just as soon as we sell one of the horses."

"Yes, ma'am." Nate smiled, enjoying her spunk and integrity. What a woman!

An exasperated breath whooshed from Hank's lungs. "But how did you pay for it?"

"That's not your worry. It's taken care of and we should have enough feed to get by for a few months until we can harvest our own hay." She glanced at Nate. "Can I depend on you to help?"

"Of course, but I'll do everything. You'll stay in the house," Nate said, realizing she was smart, too. In fact, he liked everything about this woman. She knew what needed to be done and went about tackling it in spite of gargantuan odds against her.

"Thank you." She nodded, holding her chin slightly higher. In her eyes, he saw a twinge of fear and a whole lot of courage. This little woman was a scrapper. Gentle and practical on the outside, yet made of cold, hard steel on the inside.

Hank's face reddened, and he opened his mouth and closed it several times, as if he wanted to argue. But he didn't. How could you argue with intelligent logic?

Finally, Hank turned and leaned against the railing again. Nate had to cock his head to hear his next words. "Well, Bill got the better deal."

Nate hid a smile, but he didn't laugh out loud. And that's when he realized he loved her. It struck him like lightning. He'd been wondering about his feelings since the moment he met her, but refused to believe in love at first sight. But now, he couldn't fight it. He loved her. More than his own life.

A full, joyful feeling filled his chest to overflowing. He loved this woman for the adversity she continued to face head-on and the levelheaded way she tackled her problems. He loved her for loving her father. For stepping forward and doing what had to be done. Her gentle, yet insistent, way of handling Hank's blustering temper. The way she served him nutritious meals and quietly went behind his back to take care of the ranch when he was too sick to deal with it on his own. And what's more, Nate wanted her for his own. The thought of always watching this woman from afar, yet never being able to show her how much he loved her, made his heart sink into despair. Somehow, he had to gentle and win her trust.

She might not ever be able to love any man again, but he had to try. Loving Lily was simple, but convincing her to marry him might not be so easy.

Chapter Thirteen

The truck rattled across the Bailey bridge as Dad drove them into town. Dressed in a loose-fitting flower-print dress and toeless high heels, Lily closed her eyes until they passed over the river. She hadn't yet overcome her fear from the flood and closing her eyes made it easier to bear.

As they transferred from dirt road to pavement, she turned her head and studied the red brick church from afar. She'd been home for weeks now, but finally agreed to attend church with Dad. They'd arrive for Sunday services in a matter of minutes and the tension headache she'd been fighting all morning pounded against her temples.

No doubt she knew most of the people in the congregation. What if they started asking her questions about her past? What if they wouldn't accept her? The loose dress was meant to hide her pregnancy, but it did little good. People would naturally ask about her absentee husband. The last thing she wanted was for folks to know she'd unknowingly had an affair with a married man. Nate hadn't revealed her secret, which had earned him a little more of her trust.

In Lily's book, Tommy had committed adultery. And she had unwittingly participated. She'd repented her transgressions and abandoned her old lifestyle, but she didn't feel forgiven. Maybe she never would.

"Dad, I'd rather not tell everyone I'm not married," she said.

He tossed her a frown, his blunt fingers gripping the steering wheel. He looked handsome in a western suit and turquoise bolo tie. "And just how do you propose we keep it a secret? Word has already spread through town. With your small frame, it's easy to tell you're very pregnant. If they haven't already heard, folks are bound to ask where your husband is. And then it'll come out that you don't have one."

"It's no one's business."

"That might be true, but you're gonna have to live your life. I never taught you to hide, darlin'. If you make a mistake, you make it right and move on."

His terse voice did nothing to ease her misgivings. In fact, just the opposite. How could she ever make this right? She didn't want to fling her pregnancy in everyone's face. If Dad still couldn't accept and forgive her, how would everyone at church do so?

How could God ever forgive her?

"I'm not hiding, Dad. I'm working on the Rodeo Committee and trying to help you with the ranch. I'm trying to make this right. What more do you want from me?"

His face reddened with anger and his low voice rumbled. "Nothing. I don't want one thing from you, girl. I never did."

Tears pricked the backs of her eyes. She turned away so he wouldn't see. And when he pulled into the church parking lot, he got out and turned to look at her.

"Well, are you coming in or not?" he growled.

She couldn't answer. Her throat felt like sandpaper and she swallowed back a croak of sorrow.

Dad released a giant huff of irritation, then slammed the truck door and stomped up the sidewalk. Lily sat there in the hot truck, sweat trickling down her back. Dad had taken the keys with him, so she couldn't leave and come back later to pick him up.

People gathered at the front entrance, waving and chatting. Louise Gillum, a thin woman with dark graying hair and a penchant for gossip, intercepted Dad at the door. Even though Lily couldn't hear their conversation, she could see their expressions. Dad pointed at the truck and Louise looked that way, her eyes filled with pity.

Dad went inside, and Louise clasped the arm of another woman Lily didn't recognize. Louise gestured toward Lily and tossed a disgusted glare her way.

Great! Lily couldn't go inside. She contemplated taking a long walk but feared who she might run into. She was stuck out here. But sitting inside the truck on a hot day wouldn't do her and the baby any good, either. What should she—

A tap on the window made her snap her head around. Nate stood there wearing a dark suit, white shirt and red tie. Freshly shaved, he'd combed his short hair back. With his high cheekbones and square chin, he looked like a model who had just stepped off the cover of *GQ* magazine.

A handsome heartbreaker.

He gave her an inviting smile and for a fraction of a moment, she thought she'd never been so happy to see someone in all her life.

She opened the door just a crack. "Yes?"

"What're you doing sitting here all alone in this heat?"

Cynicism threaded through her like a spiderweb and she shivered. "I...I'm not feeling well."

Okay, that was partly true, but mostly an excuse to hide.

"Where's your dad?" he asked.

"Inside."

Nate's brow furrowed as he thought this over. "I take it he's still not too accepting of your circumstance."

How did he always seem to read between the lines and make deductions with such clarity?

"Actually, I think it's me he doesn't want to accept."

"I find that hard to believe. You're his daughter."

"I think he resents me because I'm not…"

"Because you're not married."

She nodded, feeling miserable.

"One wrong choice doesn't need to ruin your life."

"But this was a doozy."

"Christ took even that burden onto himself. Because of what He did, we can all be forgiven by simply repenting."

A harsh laugh slipped from her throat. She believed what he said, yet couldn't accept it for herself. "I wish it were that simple. I haven't made just one wrong choice but a whole bevy of them."

He leaned his hip against the side of the truck. "That's the miracle of forgiveness. In return for repenting and trying to do better each time, the Lord forgets what we've done wrong. The Atonement isn't just for me and other people, Lil. It's also for you."

She folded her arms, trembling in spite of the heat. "I still don't want to get married. Not ever."

He curled his long fingers around the edge of the door. "That's reasonable, all things considered. Knowing about Tommy, I can't say I blame you."

His understanding manner put her slightly at ease.

"But what about the other side of the coin?" he asked.

She lifted her brows in question. "What other side?"

"All the good men out there who're looking for a woman to love. Someone to build a life with. Someone who adores them in return."

She snorted. "I'm not sure such men exist."

"Oh, believe me, they're out there. They're closer than you might think. You just need to know where to look."

She didn't pretend not to understand. He'd made it clear that he was interested in her. With Nate, she didn't have to play any games. Quite refreshing, considering all the lies and drama she'd gotten from Tommy.

He pulled the door wide open and reached to take her hand. "You know, sitting here in this heat won't help you feel better. Come inside and go to church with me. No one else matters."

Lily hesitated, staring at the top button of his suit coat. Oh, she was tempted by his offer. She wanted to be closer to God and realized church services could help with that. To work out her own salvation in spite of judgmental creatures who fluttered around the church waiting to focus on other people's problems. So tempted to trust this man and let him protect and defend her. Yet she didn't dare. She'd trusted before, and look where that had gotten her. No place she wanted to be.

"Come on. I won't let anyone hurt you. You'll be with me," he urged in a gentle tone.

With him. For one nanosecond, she envisioned what being with Nathan Coates might mean. Having a real, legitimate life with this man, she could almost pretend she didn't have a little problem growing inside her to deal with. If they didn't discuss the baby, it would go away. As long as Lily remained strong and calm on the outside, everything would be fine. Maybe Lily could feel normal again.

But she knew better. Fear and disparagement coiled through every fiber of her being. Putting her on constant edge. Stealing any form of happiness she might find. She only knew one thing: She was so, so very sorry for what she'd done. She wanted God's forgiveness. And she wanted to do what was right for the innocent little girl she would soon give birth to.

"If people see you with me, they'll start more gossip. They'll think you're a bad man for hanging out with a bad woman like me."

"Nonsense. People might talk, but I just don't care about

those people. There's nothing to be afraid of. Everything's gonna be all right," Nate said.

How she longed to believe him. He seemed to see right through her, into the deepest part of her soul. Right to the heart of all her insecurities.

"I don't want your pity," she said.

"And you won't get any from me. That's why I think you should get out of this truck and come into church with me." In spite of his words, his soothing voice was lulling her senses. Encouraging her to toughen up.

She took a deep, cleansing breath before hardening her jaw. "I'm not afraid."

"Of course you're not. Neither am I."

To prove it, she took his hand and slid out of the truck. His strong fingers tightened around hers, steadying her, giving her support.

A fluttering of emotion settled in her stomach. The baby gave a hard kick, as if she approved.

Nate paused, standing near enough that she caught the subtle scent of his spicy cologne. He gave a low whistle. "Wow, you look beautiful today."

A shiver of happiness swept over her. "Thank you, but I feel big as a Mack truck."

He chuckled, looking down at her tummy. "No one expects you to be skinny while you're carrying a baby, Lily. It wouldn't be healthy. You're doing just what you need to do right now. And you're the most beautiful woman I've ever met."

He cupped her cheek with his hand, his rough calluses rubbing lightly against her skin. She counted to two before she turned away. His words lightened her heart and gave her the courage to go inside, but a strange fluttering filled her chest that had nothing to do with her pregnancy.

As they walked up the sidewalk, Lily tried to tell herself

she was only drawn to this man's generosity, nothing more. The same way a stray cat is drawn to a sheltering home. It couldn't be more than that. Not for a woman like her.

"I'll be out to the ranch right after church," he said. "I can take care of the evening feeding of the horses."

"But it's the Sabbath." She didn't look at him, hyperconscious of his tall body close beside her.

"The animals need to be fed and watered even on the Sabbath."

They reached the front door. Everyone had gone inside. The meeting would begin soon. The soft chords of organ music reached her ears. A sick feeling of panic caused her stomach to churn. Prickles of alarm dotted her flesh. She pulled back, but Nate kept a gentle hold on her arm.

Reaching past her with one hand, he opened the door and whispered against her ear. "It's gonna be fine. You're not alone. You've got me and God with you."

How she hoped and prayed he was right.

He drew her inside, smiling down into her eyes. All she could see was his handsome face. As if they were the only two people in the world. Forgetting her father and the congregation inside who may or may not be happy to see her.

They stepped inside the chapel and slid into a back pew as the music stopped, the meeting just beginning. In spite of their late arrival, several people noticed them sitting close together. Heads turned their way. Only Myra and Bill Stokely smiled at her. That was something. But Lily heard the whispers and saw the nudges. The censure in people's eyes. No doubt sitting with Nate would set off a bevy of conjecture and gossip. She didn't want to ruin this good man's reputation.

She shifted nervously in her seat. "I shouldn't have come inside. I don't belong here."

He patted her hand. "Sure you do. This is the Lord's house. And He welcomes everyone. Even you and me."

Lily watched with morbid amusement as news of her presence spread like wildfire through the crowd.

She caught sight of Dad sitting on the front row. All alone. He had his head bowed, looking just as forlorn as she felt. The urge to go and join him almost overwhelmed her. She hated the thought of his sitting alone in church. Yet she was too much of a coward to walk up the middle aisle where everyone would see her. Not today anyway.

Baby steps here. She needed time to adjust. To gain strength and confidence in God's forgiveness. And to forgive herself, too.

Instead, she closed her eyes for several minutes, forcing herself to concentrate on the sermon rather than the people surrounding her. She'd made it through the front door. Surely it would get easier from here.

"You okay?" Nate asked after a moment.

She nodded her head but didn't open her eyes.

He tightened his fingers around hers and she realized he still held her hand. She almost pulled away, but couldn't bring herself to do so right now. Besides the Lord, Nate seemed her only lifeline at this point. And if she let go, she might drown in a sea of self-pity and doubt.

Chapter Fourteen

The sermon was on service to others. A topic that both shamed and inspired Lily. She thought of how much Dad, her teachers and other people had done for her in the past. And she became even more determined to begin serving others in return. Somehow her resolution buoyed her spirits and gave her added courage to move beyond her sadness. To help lift other people's loads if she could. It would take a lot of time, but she had taken the first steps toward turning her life around and she wanted to do even more.

Another thought struck her. When she served others, she was also serving God. How simple. How honest and lovely. That was what the Gospel of Christ was all about.

Only when the service ended did she finally release Nate's hand. He smiled in understanding, and clenched and released his fist several times, as if to get the blood flowing back through his fingers.

"I'm sorry," she said as she stood.

He joined her, his tall body shielding her from view of other people. "Don't be."

"Why aren't you married, Nate?" The moment the words left her mouth, she wished she could call them back. For all she knew, he'd been divorced or dumped by a woman he loved. Something painful that he didn't want to share.

"You really want to know?" he asked.

She nodded, feeling mean-spirited for asking him such a personal question. Yet his response was intensely important to her for some crazy reason.

"In the past, I've dated a lot of lovely, educated women. But I never found that one gal who really clicked with me. Someone I felt comfortable with and was easy to talk to. Someone who made me feel lighter than air. Like I couldn't draw another breath until I saw her again. In the past, I could never envision coming home every day to any of the ladies I went out with, much less raise a family with them. I guess you could say I never met the right woman…until recently."

Recently. Her heart gave a sudden lurch and she clenched her jaw. His candor left her speechless and a hollow feeling settled in her chest. "Nate, I—"

He cut her off. "You asked, so hear me out, Lily. I never knew how lonely I was until you came into my life."

Oh, she couldn't do this. He was talking about marriage, wasn't he?

"I…I can't stay for Sunday school," she said. "Next week, after the shock of my return has worn off a bit, I'll stay for all the meetings. But not today."

"That's okay. I'll take you home."

She breathed with relief as he led her toward the door. Out of the corner of her eye, she caught sight of Louise skirting through the pews, headed straight toward Lily.

Nate must have also seen Louise. He pressed Lily ahead of him, cutting Louise off as they stepped outside into the fresh air.

"I'm parked over there. Go on and get inside my truck. I'll be there shortly." With the palm of his hand, Nate pushed against Lily's lower back and indicated his truck sitting beneath a cherry tree in full blossom.

Lily hurried in that direction, conscious of Nate turning and intercepting Louise with a congenial smile.

"Hi, Louise. How are you?" he said.

Lily glanced over her shoulder and saw Louise craning her head around Nate, trying to get past him. "I'm fine. Is that Lily Hansen I just saw?"

"Yes, as a matter of fact, it is."

Clara came outside and joined them, but Lily kept going. "Hi, Nate. Is Lily leaving?"

As Lily reached Nate's truck, she heard his deep voice behind. "She's not feeling well, so I'm taking her home."

Home. Nate was taking her there. And somehow, that thought frightened Lily more than anything else. Because something had just happened without her even being able to stop it. Without her even realizing it until it had already occurred. Nate had shielded her without her asking him to. Since their first meeting, he'd become her protector. He'd said he wanted to be more than just friends. At first, she'd been suspicious of his motives. Now she believed he was a genuinely kind man. But did he really care for her? Or did he just feel sorry for her?

Lily didn't know what to make of this. She couldn't completely push Nate away, yet she couldn't let him get close, either. Could she?

Nate walked down the front steps of the church house and reached the sidewalk with Louise and Clara in hot pursuit. He turned and lifted his hands in the air, hoping to ward them off. "Ladies, you can speak with Lily another time. Right now, I'm taking her home. She doesn't feel well."

"I'm sorry to hear that. Thank you for taking care of her, Nate." Clara stopped and gave him an understanding smile.

"But...but I was hoping to talk to her," Louise said.

Nate nodded. "And I'm sure she wants to talk to you, too, but maybe next week."

The woman's small eyes narrowed like a hawk's. "I heard she's pregnant."

Nate bit his tongue, wishing the old biddy would leave Lily alone.

"She is expecting a baby. Isn't that wonderful news?" Clara said.

Louise leaned closer and spoke in a mock whisper that anyone passing by would be able to hear. She eyed Nate. "Do you know who the father is? She's not married."

"I don't think it's our business, do you?" Clara asked.

"Well, I just think it's—"

Nate took a step, the woman's needling voice raising the hackles on the back of his neck. The urge to strangle Louise filled his entire being. Lily had been deeply hurt by Tommy and Nate promised himself no one would hurt her like that again.

Clara's features tightened and she lifted a hand in dismissal. "I wouldn't pay attention to mindless gossip, Louise. It's not our business nor our place to judge. By the way, how is your son doing in San Quentin?"

Oh, that was a low blow, but it shut Louise up. Nate knew she had a son in prison for armed robbery. So who was Louise to find fault with Lily? Nate almost hugged Clara for her quick comeback. Instead, he winked at her. In return, she gave him a quiet smile. Whether Lily believed it, she had friends here in Jasper. People who actually loved and cared for her.

People like him.

The thought of loving Lily Hansen almost sizzled Nate's toes. He was highly conscious of her as a beautiful, intelligent woman. And whether she liked it, he wanted her for his own.

"My…my son is just fine. He gets out in sixteen months. I wanted to throw a baby shower for Lily," Louise said.

Clara shook her head. "As her best friend since childhood, I've already asked to do that."

Without a backward glance, Nate sauntered toward his truck. Grateful to Clara for intervening and giving him the time to get Lily out of here. He perked his ears for the sound of following feet behind him and breathed a sigh of relief when he didn't hear it. Finally, Louise had gotten the hint.

Without fanfare, Nate opened the door and climbed into the driver's seat of his truck. Lily sat in the passenger seat, her face void of color, her shoulders squared and tense.

"You okay?" he asked.

She nodded, her voice sounding small. "I suppose everyone at church knows about the baby."

He inserted the key into the ignition. "Yes, but you knew that before you came here. There's no way to keep it quiet."

She lifted a hand to rest across her rounding stomach, her eyes wistful. "Dad won't know what happened to me."

Nate nodded toward the church house where Hank stood on the front steps talking to Clara and Louise. "I'm sure Clara will tell him I took you home."

Putting the truck in gear, he backed it up and drove out of the parking lot. He glanced at Lily as he thought about what he wanted to say to her. An idea had started forming in his mind days ago and now he was trying to get up the courage to tell Lily about it.

"You have a good friend in Clara Richens," he said.

"Oh?"

"She just put Louise in her place." He told Lily what Clara had done.

Lily nodded. "Clara always was quite blunt. I never had her courage."

"Yes, you do. In your own way. You just go about things a

bit differently, but I don't think I've ever met anyone as courageous as you."

Her mouth softened and she looked at him with a mixture of gratitude or doubt, he wasn't sure which.

"Yes, I believe Clara is a true friend. She never criticized or betrayed me when we were kids. And she's been kind to me since I returned home."

"I'm glad you have someone to talk to."

When they reached the outskirts of town, he turned left, heading up to Angel Lake instead of south toward Emerald Ranch.

"Where are you going?" Lily laid her hand along the arm rest of the door as she looked out the windshield.

"I thought we'd take a little ride. Is that okay?"

She nodded, her expression serene.

The road twined up the Ruby Mountains, the truck finally emerging past a subalpine dwarf aspen forest area. Nate eyed the remains of an avalanche from the past winter, extending across the valley for several miles. Gigantic drifts of dirty snow still covered the road in places.

"I'm afraid this is as far as we dare go today," he said.

"Wow! Look at that mound of dirt blocking the road." Lily pointed at a huge pile of trees and rocks sealed in a mound of damp sludge.

"Yep, I've scheduled a road crew to clear it away before the Fourth of July weekend. Campers will want to get through and won't be able to."

"I've never seen anything like it. Did the flooding cause this?"

"No, this was caused by an avalanche."

She frowned and gazed at him with contemplation. "Is this another debris torrent building up?"

"Kind of, but different. This one doesn't have any water

backing up behind it. The debris dam building up above Bill's ranch included the force of water."

Lily shuddered and Nate thought she might be remembering the flash flood that almost killed her. She'd learned the hard way that water could be a strong and ruthless assailant.

He gazed at the tidy campground next to the lake, flanked by glacial cirques. This was part of his ranger district and he took any and all opportunities to ensure all was well.

He parked near a picnic table and got out, going around to open Lily's door for her.

"I'm not dressed for hiking," she said.

Nate heard the tension in her voice. He glanced at her pretty high heels and trim ankles. A feeling of masculine appreciation zinged through him and he longed to take her into his arms and kiss her sweet lips. Instead, he indicated his nice suit. "I'm not, either. We won't go very far. Just to the tables where we can sit and enjoy the view."

He cupped her elbow as he led her across the rocky ground. Whipping out his kerchief, he laid it across the seat so she wouldn't snag or get her dress dirty. Then he sat opposite of her, gazing at the crystal water and jagged rocks.

"In the wintertime, this is a dangerous avalanche area."

"Yes, I remember one year some of my friends from school came up here on snowmobiles. One of the kids was killed in an avalanche. It took several months to find his body. It broke his parents' hearts." She shivered.

"Are you cold?" Nate leaned his elbows on the table, his gaze pinned on her face.

"No. I was just remembering that gloomy time. It is lovely here. One of my favorite places on earth."

"Mine, too." He smiled, trying to put her at ease.

A solitary tear dripped onto her cheek and Nate reached across the table to wipe it away with his thumb. "Don't be sad, Lil. It's not the end of the world. There are happier days ahead for you."

"I'm just thinking how much I have to be grateful for. Dad's a stern man, but he never gave up on me."

"Neither did the Lord."

She nodded in agreement.

He took a deep, cleansing breath. "I've been wanting to talk with you about something I've had on my mind for days now."

"And what's that?"

"I meant it when I said I've never met the right woman for me...until recently." He reached into his pants pocket and knelt on one knee beside her. She looked so beautiful in her flowered dress, the afternoon breeze rustling her long curls.

Holding up his arm, he opened his hand to reveal a large diamond engagement ring resting on his palm. "Lil, this is yours. I'd like to return it to you."

Lily gasped, staring at the ring in silenced amazement. In her eyes, Nate saw recognition.

"That...that's my mother's engagement ring."

"Yes, I know. I'd like you to wear it again. I want you to marry me and be my wife."

"Nate, I...I'm pregnant."

He gave a low laugh and inclined his head. "Yes, I'm well aware of that. I'd like you to be my wife and I want to be a father to your baby."

"But...but how did you get Mom's ring? I sold it to pay for hay."

"And I bought it back to return to you."

Her brown eyes glistened with moisture. Ah, did she have to cry? He wanted this to be a happy time. But she wasn't happy. In fact, she looked heartbroken.

Tears of indignity fell freely down her cheeks and her face contorted in frustration. "You shouldn't have done that, Nate."

"I wanted to. More than anything else in the world, I want you to be happy." He handed her a tissue from his pocket. "Don't cry, honey. Smile for me instead."

She cried harder, biting her top lip, looking down at the ground as she struggled to regain her composure.

Nate realized what he said was true. Yes, it was way too soon to be asking her to marry him. Yes, he should wait and court her and give them more time to get to know one another. But in spite of all that, he loved this woman. If he waited, she might give the baby up for adoption. She might leave and he'd never find her. And Nate didn't want that. He wanted to keep this child. To become a real family.

To be a father and husband.

Taking Lily's hand, he slid the oversize diamond ring onto her finger and gazed into her eyes with all the love he had shining in his heart. "Marry me, Lily. Marry me and make me the happiest man on earth."

Chapter Fifteen

❧

"No, I can't marry you, Nate. I can't." Lily tugged off her mother's ring and handed it back to him, but he didn't take it. Instead, he came to his feet and placed his hands in his pants pockets.

"Why? Why not?"

"I don't want your pity."

"I don't want to marry you out of pity, Lil. Surely you know me well enough to know that."

"No, I don't. I…I'm soiled goods."

A spark of pain flashed in his eyes and Lily hated herself for hurting him. This man who had been so kind and generous to her. So easy to talk to. Always there. Always protecting her. And look how she treated him in return.

He shook his head, his gaze never wavering from hers. "Not to me, you're not. You're beautiful, kind, generous, hardworking, and the only woman I've ever wanted to be with."

Was he a masochist? What man wanted to marry a woman like her? Marrying her could taint his reputation and destroy his career with the Forest Service. "You deserve so much more. I…I don't love you, Nate."

He jerked one shoulder in a shrug, his face stoic with resolve. "I love you enough for both of us, Lily."

"But that's not enough for me. And it wouldn't be fair to you."

A troubled frown pulled at his brows. "Why don't you let me be the judge of that?"

"You don't understand."

"You're right. I don't understand your reluctance. But I can offer you everything you've ever wanted. Security. Reliability. And love."

"I do want those things, Nate, but I'm not willing to just take and give nothing in return. I can't marry someone I don't love. I won't marry someone because he feels sorry for me."

"But I don't—"

She stopped him. She couldn't stand the thought of seeing this big, strong man begging. "No, Nate. You have my answer and that's final."

This was about pity and nothing more. Nate must be insane. Or very kind and generous. Which wasn't a good reason to marry someone.

She held out her hand, trying to give him back the ring, but he lowered his hands out of her grasp.

He stared at her, his dark eyes not filled with pain and anger as she expected, but rather compassion. "Keep it. I know how much it means to you. I want you to have it."

He backed away. She followed him, holding the ring out. As much as she loved this diamond and what it meant to her, she couldn't keep it. It didn't belong to her now.

"Nate, it's not mine anymore." When he wouldn't take it, she dropped it into the pocket of his suit coat and stepped away, folding her arms tight over the top of her tummy.

He lowered one of his calloused hands and folded his palm over his pocket, as though feeling the weight of the ring inside. He stared at the lake, his face devoid of expression. Only the subtle stiffness of his back and shoulders told her how upset he was.

He turned abruptly, his eyes filled with determination. He lifted his hands and took a step toward her.

"Don't! Don't touch me." She backed away fast, holding up her hands, as if that could ward him off. A blaze of hot panic shot through her, stinging her skin. Injecting her body with adrenalin. Her survival instincts kicked into high gear and she cried out.

Nate hesitated, standing just inches away. Confusion crossed his features and he took another step.

With a strangled cry, Lily turned and ran toward the truck. She couldn't let him hit her. Couldn't let him harm her baby.

"Lil, wait!"

She stumbled over the uneven ground. Her ankle twisted in her high heels and she almost went down but caught her balance just in time. She limped the rest of the way, hurrying as fast as she could go. Seeking the protection of the vehicle.

"Don't run, honey. You'll fall." Nate's cautionary voice came from behind, urgent yet gentle.

She reached the truck. Her fingers jerked at the doorknob. Pulling hard. She had to get inside. Had to be where it was safe.

The handle jerked back, stinging her fingers. Locked! She whirled around, pressing her back against the hard metal of the truck. Panting. Frightened as she faced Nate and what his big, strong fists might do to her.

"Please, don't," she croaked, shrinking away.

Through her tears, she watched him with dread. Bracing herself for the exploding pain. Folding her arms across her stomach, knowing it wasn't enough to protect her child if Nate decided to hit or kick her.

He stood in front of her, his eyes filled with concern and sadness. He lifted his hands, palms facing her. His voice sounded thick with conviction and he backed away several paces. "I won't ever hurt you, Lil. You needn't fear me. Not ever."

She pressed a hand to her mouth, with nowhere to run. Sobbing. Trembling. A prayer in her heart.

Please help me, God.

Nate's voice was whisper soft and filled with anguish. "Lily. Oh, sweet Lily. What did he do to you? What did he do?"

Nothing! Everything! How she wished she could confide in Nate. To tell him what she'd been through. To learn how to trust again. But she couldn't. The price was too high.

Nate stepped back even farther, his eyes full of pain. "I'm not Tommy. I'll never raise a hand to you in anger. Not ever. This I vow."

His soft voice surrounded her with firm conviction. How she wished she could believe him. Between Tommy's violence and Dad's explosive anger, she'd been trained over the years not to trust men. Trust was a luxury she couldn't afford anymore. But how could she explain her skepticism to Nate? He'd done nothing but show her kindness.

"Are you okay now?" he asked. Still a soft voice. Still soothing and gentle.

She wiped her eyes and nodded, a small shudder running through her body. He must think she was crazy. A raving lunatic. "I…I'm so sorry, Nate. I guess I lost it there for a moment."

"Can I come closer?" he asked.

She eyed his tall body, dressed in his best Sunday suit. She saw no harsh lines on his face. No reddening with anger. No tense shoulders or clenched fists. But body language wasn't always a good indicator of intentions. Tommy had been calm and serene one moment, and explosive with fury the next. She'd learned to have quick reflexes, just in case.

She nodded.

Nate stepped close enough to touch her. She watched him, ready to spring away if he even flinched.

"Talk to me, Lil. Please. I want to be close to you. I'll never betray you. You can trust me."

Trust was the last thing she was prepared to give. And yet she wanted it so much. Just one friend in the whole wide world she could tell everything to. Hold nothing back. Nate had been so kind. So good. Surely she could confide in him, couldn't she?

"I…I almost lost this baby once, Nate."

"Because of Tommy?"

She nodded, pressing her left hand against the side of her stomach, her right hand ready to push him away if necessary.

Nate squeezed his eyes tightly closed, as if he could feel her pain. When he opened them again, she saw nothing but compassion and a bit of fury there. "I'm so sorry, Lily. I wish I'd been there to protect you."

Did he mean it? "How could you? We didn't know each other yet and it wasn't your job."

"I still wish I'd been there. I would have knocked Tommy senseless for ever hurting you. Believe me, I'd have taught him a hard lesson."

Even though it might not be Christian, she kind of liked that thought.

"Thanks. Tommy always had a bad temper. He'd slap me sometimes, but when I confronted him over his wife and kids, he…he beat me up pretty bad. I spent two weeks in the hospital. While I was there, I discovered I was pregnant. I thanked God that Tommy hadn't killed my baby."

She swallowed around a sudden lump in her throat. A fresh welling of tears sprang into her eyes. Her chin quivered, but she bit her lip, refusing to give in to the emotions trying to overcome her.

Nate shifted his feet, his hands seeming restless, as though he longed to take her into his arms and hold her. "I'm so sorry, Lil. If you were mine, I'd love and cherish you. I'd protect you."

Did he mean it? She longed to believe him. To trust him. "But you see why I…I can't marry you, Nate?"

He shook his head. "No, I don't see that at all. All I see is a beautiful, heartbroken woman who needs a good man to show her that real love isn't made up of lies and violence. It's made up of trust and respect."

"You can't possibly love me, Nate. We barely know each other. I have yet to meet a man who knows what real love is."

"Until now," he said. "I'm that man, Lily. I won't give up on you. Or us. Not ever."

"I'm not sure I even know what real love is, Nate."

An understanding smile curved Nate's full lips. "You know, I've discovered that most of the time we're harder on ourselves than God is. He wants us to be happy. Knowing how much God loves us, how can we withhold forgiveness from ourselves? If we really understand that the Lord wants to forgive us, it makes it a bit easier to forgive ourselves."

She thought this over. Although she knew they never could be together, in her heart of hearts, she couldn't help wishing things could be different. "I wish I'd met you years ago, before I met Tommy and totally messed up my life."

He smiled at her, the sun gleaming against his dark hair. His eyes brightened and she thought he must be the most handsome man she'd ever seen.

"It's not too late," he said. "Your life isn't messed up. I just wish I could convince you how wonderful things could be for us. We could start fresh. I'm willing to try, if you are."

She bit her lip, longing to take the step he wanted from her. But she couldn't. She'd promised herself and the Lord that she'd never jump into another relationship again. That she'd do what was right for this baby, no matter how much it hurt.

And right now, she believed giving her baby up for adoption was the best thing. Even so, Nate's words left her shaken to the core. For one second, she could envision them married and raising this baby together. Having more children later on down the road. Working together. Being a genuine, happy family.

She turned toward the truck, not quite taking her eyes off him. "Will you unlock the door, please?"

She heard a chirp as he pressed the key fob for the automatic locks. He reached past her to open the door. She let him hold her elbow as she got inside. Moving slow, she eased the seat belt across her tummy and sat back while he clicked it into place. When he looked into her eyes, he smiled, their noses mere inches apart. Right now, when she was lucid, she wondered how she could ever be frightened of this good man.

The warmth of his breath whispered past her lips as he spoke. "I'm not giving up on us. When you're ready, I'll be here for you. Forever."

A century seemed to pass as they gazed at each other. A time she would cherish until the day she died. Because this was the first time, the first man, to ever tell her he loved her without demanding something in return.

When he pulled away, he brushed her hand with his. No grasping or holding tight. Just a gentle touch of his fingertips. Soft and yearning. Building trust between them in spite of her insistence that they could never be more than friends.

As Nate drove her home, he talked about his work. Dirt roads that needed rebuilding later in the summer, after the flooding had passed. High mountain pastures he was opening up for new grazing permittees to use. Leasing National Forest land for possible geothermal development.

"Geothermal development could be a good form of green energy as well as an opportunity to help create jobs for the State of Nevada," he said.

Lily let him talk, letting his deep, calm voice soothe her

jangled nerves. She caught the enthusiasm in his tone and realized this man loved and knew his job well. He was so much more than just a horse trainer.

"Your job sounds complicated. How have you learned all of this stuff?" she asked.

He shrugged. "I have a bachelor's in range management and a dual master's degree in soil science and hydrology, along with eleven years' experience. There's still a lot I need to learn, but I love what I do."

"You love working with horses, too."

He inclined his head. "Most people are good at a lot of things."

She snorted. "Not me. I'm good at working on a ranch and that's about it."

"You're also a great cook. You forget I've eaten a few meals at your house. You make the best homemade rolls I've ever had. None better."

His praise touched her deeply. It'd been a long time since she felt good at anything. "Mom taught me."

"And you're good with horses, too. I saw how you handled Misty. As soon as you have this little girl, we'll get you back in the saddle. Then you can show me what else you can do."

Lily pressed the palms of her hands against her baby bump, longing to raise her child with all the love and gentleness she should have been raised with.

"I used to dream of going to college one day," she said.

"There's no reason you can't still do that."

"I can't leave Emerald Ranch as long as Dad needs me."

He hunched his shoulders. "Online classes work you just as hard as in-class instruction. Why not go to college online?"

She laughed. "I wonder what Dad would say if I asked him to buy a computer and have a line strung to our house so we can have internet connection."

"He'd do it in a heartbeat."

Lily had her doubts.

"It's small, but we have a library in town where you can do research for your studies," he said. "You can order in a book from numerous universities around the nation if you need it. Even if it's just one class at a time, you'd be surprised how quickly the classes add up. School is hard, but well worth it. And there's nothing wrong with being an educated rancher."

A glow of pleasure filled her chest. His words encouraged and gave her hope. For the first time in a long time, she actually thought about tackling her education again. One class at a time.

When Nate drove the truck into the yard at Emerald Ranch, the colts and fillies raced across the paddock. They waved their heads over the fence, their ears pricked forward.

"Look at those silly kids. You're spoiling them. They want their molasses treats," Lily said.

"Yeah, the big babies. They'll get their treats as long as they perform their training well."

Lily laughed. In such a short time, the horses had come to love and trust Nate. So why couldn't she do the same?

He killed the motor and looked at her, a soft smile creasing his mouth. "You should do that more often."

"What?"

"Laugh out loud."

Nate got out and opened her door for her. As she stepped down, he backed away. Not too far. Just enough so he didn't touch her. And she realized he was doing it on purpose. To show her that he meant no harm.

"I'll tell you what, sunshine. I'll make you a promise right now."

She tilted her head, looking at him with curiosity. "And what's that?"

"I promise to make you laugh every time I see you."

"That might be kind of nice," she admitted.

"I'll see you later this afternoon. I'll be back to feed and water the horses."

"You don't need to come back. I can do it—"

He walked around the truck, cutting her off, his voice insistent. "I'll be back later. I just made you a promise and I intend to keep it."

He got in the truck, then waited until she was safely inside the house before pulling away. Lily continued to stare out the window at him, even when all she could see was the dust rising from the dirt road to show his passing.

Thankfully, Dad wasn't home from church yet. Seeking solace, Lily went into her room and lay across her bed. She searched the worn pages of her mom's Scriptures and meditated on what had happened today. She couldn't reconcile why, but Nate made her feel both safe and lonely all at the same time. And yet, when she'd rejected his marriage proposal, she'd gone berserk, thinking he might hurt her.

Even prayer didn't help and she found herself troubled by his marriage proposal. It'd be so easy to say yes and become his wife and let him help bear her burdens. But she couldn't do that. She had to resolve her own problems first.

In the fifteenth chapter of Luke, she read about the prodigal son returning to his father after sinning against Heaven. And the father told his other son: *Be glad, for this thy brother was dead, and is alive again; and was lost, and is found.*

Surely Lily was the prodigal daughter returned after almost destroying her life. She didn't have a jealous sibling to contend with, but she had her own demons to overcome. Her soul had been so very lost. And somehow, out of the muck and mire of transgression, the Lord had found and brought her home.

So if God could forgive her, why couldn't she forgive herself?

She laid her head against a pillow and pressed her hands against her abdomen. The baby's strong kicks thumped against her rib cage and she laughed, her eyes filling with tears of joy. How she loved this innocent little child. And for several fleeting seconds, she longed to share these sweet moments with Nate. To let him keep his promise to make her laugh every time she saw him.

To fall in love and marry him.

When he returned to the ranch later that afternoon, she stayed inside the house. Instead, Dad went outside to the barn. She just couldn't face Nate again so soon. She had a lot to think about and even more to sort out. Because against her better judgment, she was actually entertaining the thought of staying at Emerald Ranch for good.

Chapter Sixteen

The next morning, Lily drove into town to meet with Clara at her house. The white double-wide manufactured home didn't speak of great wealth, but that had never mattered to Lily. A short, chain-link fence surrounded the yard of green grass with purple-and-pink petunias filling the front flower beds.

Clara greeted her with a warm hug and brought her inside. Sitting at the kitchen table, they drank iced sodas. Clara bounced Sandy, her eight-month-old baby girl, on her knee as they jotted down plans for ushers at the rodeo. The gurgling baby waved her tiny arms and Lily was enthralled, hardly able to believe she would soon be a mother, too.

"You're getting big." Clara nodded at Lily's tummy with a knowing smile.

"Yes, I still have another month to go, but I'm ready for this baby to be born now." Lily's throat tightened and she struggled to swallow. How would she ever be able to give up her baby? It'd be the hardest thing she'd ever done in her life.

"Don't worry. That'll change soon enough, and then you'll have a bawling baby to deal with."

Not if she gave the baby away.

"Have you spoken with Nate about security?"

"Yes, we've talked in the evenings when he comes to the ranch to train the horses."

"Good. We always have to deal with a few drunk and disorderly people at the rodeo. By the way, what's the deal with you and Nate?" Clara asked.

Lily tensed. Had Nathan told anyone that he'd proposed? "What do you mean?"

"You two looked awfully chummy at church. You're a cute couple."

"We aren't a couple." The ice chinked inside Lily's glass as she took a sip of soda.

"Before he whisked you away in his truck, he looked ready to throttle Louise Gillum. That woman makes me so mad. She's such a busybody."

Knowing how he'd defended her made Lily feel even worse for hurting him yesterday. "He was just being kind."

Clara snorted. "Honey, believe me, I can recognize the difference between a man being kind and a man in love. Nate has all the symptoms of being completely smitten with you."

Lily busied herself jotting down notes. "He'll get over it. They always do."

"Are you kidding? Not this man. He's never really dated much since he came to town a few years ago. And he's got a good reputation for honesty and reliability. He's not like your other men, Flower."

Her other men. Womanizers. Out-of-work cowboys. Rodeo bums. Liars and adulterers. But knowing Nate was the complete opposite of such men didn't make it any easier.

"He's definitely good with horses and he's a good forest ranger, too," Lily conceded.

And kind, handsome, self-assured, a hard worker and generous to a fault.

"So what do you think about him?" Clara persisted.

"I…I like him well enough, but…" After watching Clara

put Louise in her place, Lily believed she could confide in her girlhood friend.

"But what?"

"He…he asked me to marry him, Clara. He claims he loves me."

Lily still couldn't believe it. How could Nate love her enough to marry her and provide a name for her unborn child when the baby wasn't even his? She didn't understand it. It just didn't make sense.

Clara sat back in her chair with a thump and lifted the baby to her shoulder. Her gaze pinned Lily to the core, her mouth dropping open in surprise. "Well, I'll be. And what did you say?"

Lily cupped her face in her hands, her words muffled. "I told him no."

"Why?" The word burst from Clara's mouth like a nuclear explosion and the baby jerked. And then, more quietly, Clara continued. "Why would you do that?"

Lily rested her hands across her stomach and stared at the table. "Because I can't. It wouldn't be fair to Nate. It'd be a marriage of convenience and nothing more. I can't saddle him with a child that isn't even his."

"Why not? He knows what he's getting himself into. He's a big boy. Why can't you marry him?"

Lily released a pensive sigh. In a soft whisper, she told Clara everything about Tommy and almost losing the baby. "Maybe not now, but years down the road, Nate would remember that he hadn't fathered my child and he'd come to resent me. Maybe even hate me. And what about my baby? I can't put this little girl through that. She deserves a mother and father who will love her unconditionally."

Clara leaned Sandy back and gave her a bottle. "Have you contacted an adoption agency yet?"

"Not yet." She just hadn't been able to bring herself to do it, but she would. Soon.

"Are you sure that's what you want to do?" Clara asked.

"What I want is not as important as what's right for this baby. I have to put my own selfish desires on hold."

"And you think it's selfish to keep your baby?"

"It is if I can't give her a good life and raise her to be a good person."

"Why do you believe complete strangers can love your child, but Nate can't? Hundreds of people adopt sweet children they love every bit as much as they would a biological child. I have a cousin who has two adopted children and, believe me, there is absolutely no difference. They even look alike. Love knows no boundaries, Lily. Love makes everything possible. It's the only thing that really matters in life."

"Love didn't work for Tommy and me."

Clara pursed her lips. "I think that's because he had a complication called a wife and kids. He had no business lying to you. That's not love at all. A man like Tommy should never be allowed around women, children or small animals, either."

Lily agreed and it stung to realize Tommy had never loved her. Not really. "But Nate would always know he married me, saddled with someone else's child."

Lily would have laughed if the situation wasn't so sad. "I just don't see how Nate could love me and my baby the way you and Michael love each other."

"And you think giving your baby up for adoption to complete strangers would be better? No matter what, that little girl isn't going to get her real father, Lily." Clara pointed at Lily's large stomach. "Now that I know what was going on, I would never let you go back to that horrible Tommy, even if he got a divorce. He'll have a lot to explain to the Lord one day."

"Don't worry, I won't go back to him. I can't subject myself or my child to that horror ever again." Not now that God had helped her finally break the cycle of abuse.

"Then wouldn't it be better to marry Nate and keep your baby? You could be genuinely happy for the first time in your life. And he'd get to marry the woman he loves."

"But I don't think I love him."

"You don't think?"

Lily sighed, feeling confused. "I don't know anything anymore."

Clara's breath left her in a quick whoosh. Here it was. The real crux of the problem. Even eight months ago, Lily might have married a man like Nate without thinking twice about how she felt about him. But now, she wanted to do what was right. Not what was convenient or easy. And marrying Nate without knowing deep in her heart that she loved him unconditionally wasn't fair to anyone. Especially him.

"Nate deserves a woman who adores him," Lily said.

"I agree. But he's a very handsome, good man, with a lot of fine qualities. You don't think you could ever love him?"

"I don't know. I'm not sure I know what real love is." A harsh laugh slid from Lily's throat. "He barely knows me, Clara. He can't love me this soon."

"Oh, I don't know. It was love at first sight for Michael and me."

"Really?"

"Sure. The first moment we laid eyes on each other, we were crazy about one another. Even though I got pregnant, we didn't have to get married. I could have considered adoption and gone on my merry way. But our feelings for each other haven't changed in all these years. We love each other through thick and thin. We always have."

"And you think Nate loved me at first sight?"

Clara nodded. "You can see it in his eyes, Lily. He lights up like a road flare every time you're around. You're so suspicious of every man who looks your way that you can't see what real affection is anymore. And I've got news for you, girl. This is not just a simple case of the hots. Nate isn't a young kid who might be having a crush. He's a fully grown, mature man who knows how to handle himself and knows what he wants out of life. And right now, he wants you."

Oh, boy! This was a hard pill for Lily to swallow. If Nate really did love her, then he must be hurting so much after her refusal. How could they continue to work together every day under such conditions? Eating dinner each night in her kitchen. Training, feeding and cleaning up after the horses.

"Maybe Nate's feelings will soon change and he won't love me anymore," Lily said.

Clara laughed. "We're talking about Nate, not Tommy. Maybe you're the one who will change. You could realize you've been waiting all your life for a man like Nate."

Not likely.

She needed Nate's help, now more than ever. They were making great progress with several of the colts and should be able to sell several of them within the next month for a tidy sum. Lily was counting on that money to help get her and Dad caught up on their bills. Nate could recoup his money by selling her mother's engagement ring. But without Nate, she and Dad would soon fall right back into financial duress.

Besides, the thought of never seeing Nate again filled Lily with utter and deep despair. If she didn't love him, why would she feel that way? Why did she care about hurting him?

"What are you gonna do?" Clara asked.

Lily shook her head, feeling awful for hurting Nate. "I don't know. I just don't know anymore."

The first day of the town rodeo went well enough. The small motel in town had booked to capacity. Horse trailers pulled by trucks with camper shells filled the mobile home park on the edge of town. Lily sat in the stands with Dad, watching the barrel racing, roping and bronc riding as long as she could stand the heat. Then Nate insisted she go home to rest until later that evening.

"I've got this under control," he said with a smile. "Between your ushers and my security force, we can handle any fights that break out or if we have any drunk and disorderlies."

"You sure?" she asked, exhausted by the dry, sun-soaked air.

"I'm positive. But be back by seven o'clock. Clara invited me to show Toots in a cutting exhibition. It's good advertisement for the horses we're training and I don't want you to miss the show."

That sounded nice. Lily couldn't believe the good work Nate had done with the little mare. Toots had become a highly skilled cutter and Dad had started filling out entrance applications for a number of upcoming competitions.

When Lily arrived back at the rodeo grounds at a quarter to seven, she sat with Dad in a shaded are of the stands and waited. Dust rose into the air as the crews working the corrals released twenty head of cows into the arena. Over the amplifier, the speaker announced Nate's exhibition. Wearing leather chaps, boots and spurs, Nate rode out on Toots. Gone was the forest ranger she'd come to respect, replaced by a lean cowboy in full regalia.

A buzzer sounded and Lily leaned forward, her gaze pinned on Nate as he casually walked Toots through the herd of cattle. The cows milled about, moving aside to let the horse and rider through. One heifer became isolated and scampered to rejoin the herd. And that's when Nate tapped the horse with his heels and Toots went into action. Working low, the horse kept her eyes on the cow. Anticipating every move the bovine might make, Toots turned, made quick starts and stops, maneuvering herself so the cow couldn't get past. Nate simply sat on the horse, as though he were an appendage of the animal rather than a separate entity. Only when Nate gave a subtle signal did Toots allow the cow to return to the herd.

The multitude of spectators cheered. A feeling of pride and happiness rose in Lily's chest. In a short time, Nate had taken a good little filly and turned her into an amazing cow horse.

Dad whooped and hollered, his buoyant laughter joining the yells of the crowd. "Now, that's what I'm talking about."

Lily chuckled, glad to see Dad so happy.

Nate whisked the cowboy hat from his head and waved it to the crowd.

The announcer gave a shrill whistle across the PA system. "Good show! Don't you all wish that pretty little mare belonged to you, folks? If you're interested, Nathan Coates is the trainer and Lily Hansen is the owner."

Lily turned to stare at Dad. "Why did they name me as the owner?"

"Because I told them to, darlin'. I'm just staying for room and board. The ranch and horses belong to you now. I had Earl Tippens finalize my will the week after you came home. It's all legal and final. So if you leave now, you're leaving everything."

Sudden tears burned Lily's eyes. She loved Dad. More than she could ever say.

"Dad, I don't want anything from you." Her voice sounded hoarse to her own ears and she cleared the emotion clogging her throat.

He nudged her arm. Such a small, insignificant gesture, and yet it meant so much to her.

"I know that, darlin'. But you're my little girl. Now, watch what comes next."

Lily turned her attention back to the arena. She widened her eyes when Nate rode out on Peg. He loped the stallion around the arena, skirting past the cluster of cattle. Then, he stopped the horse and removed Peg's halter.

Lily gasped, thinking Nate had lost his mind. Without the halter on, Peg was in control, not Nate.

"We've got a world champion here, folks. You ever seen a cutter work without a halter?" the announcer asked over the PA system.

With a subtle nudge of his heels, Nate urged Peg into the herd of cows. Walking slow, the horse selected another beef to segregate from the herd. And then Lily gaped wide-eyed. When the cow tried to get back to the herd, Nate merely sat on the horse's back while the animal swerved, lunged and turned to keep the beef isolated. Peg did all the work. Nate simply held on to the saddle horn. The crowd went wild. Peg needed no guidance from Nate. He did his job and did it well. Showing the spectators exactly why he was a world champion.

"Wow!" Lily couldn't believe her eyes.

"Yeah, I know what you mean," Dad chuckled. "But I can't say it's easy for me to watch another man riding my horse. I wish I could ride like I used to, but it feels good to see Peg performing again."

A warm feeling of love and admiration flooded Lily's chest. "You trained Peg, Daddy. You made that horse a world champion."

"Yep, but I'm so glad you and Nate are here to help me run the ranch."

His gratitude warmed her heart.

The buzzer sounded and Nate reached down and patted Peg on the neck. The horse immediately withdrew, letting the cow return to the herd.

Nate had become more than just a horse trainer. As Lily gazed at the man who had turned her life upside down, her throat tightened and she couldn't help feeling beyond pleased by his accomplishment. He'd more than blessed their lives.

Because of him, they now had Toots. A cutting horse who would bring them a tidy sum in contest wins.

For several moments, Lily felt blue as the Pacific Ocean. How she wished Nate would stop pursuing her so she could stop hurting him. Telling him no and pushing him away had gotten harder for Lily. She just didn't want to do it anymore. It seemed she was doomed to have nothing but sad relationships all her life.

Chapter Seventeen

Nate refused to give up on Lily, despite how she'd hidden inside the house when he'd returned the night before to work with the horses. Despite her insistence that she couldn't have a relationship with another man.

Yes, her refusal cut him deep, but he never gave up once he'd set his mind on something. All his life he'd searched for one woman to make his own. One woman to make his heart sing. And he'd never found her.

Until now.

A feeling of recognition and warmth had settled in Nate's heart. Every time he saw Lily, he felt as if she were an old friend. Someone he could confide in. Someone to depend on.

Someone to adore.

Now he just needed to convince Lily that he was the man for her. And so, he came up with a plan. One that included stealth and subterfuge if necessary. He'd court Lily the old-fashioned way. And be so persistent and gentle that he'd wear down her resistance and she'd have to give in to him.

As he pulled his truck into the yard at Emerald Ranch, he saw Hank riding a large tractor, disking one of the fields in preparation for planting alfalfa. The blades gouged the fertile soil, making a thin cloud of dust rise into the air. As soon as Nate spoke with Lily, he'd go help Hank. Then he'd work with Misty and the other mares.

Nate glanced at the secret weapon he had resting beside him on the seat. A dozen red roses wrapped in green tissue paper. Even if Lily tossed them into the garbage can, he would present them to her and ask her out on a real date. If that didn't work, he'd buy her chocolates. He'd show her that she could depend on him. He'd woo her slowly. As long as it took.

As he stepped out of the truck, Beans came running from the backyard, his tongue lolling out of his mouth in a panting grin. Nate bent over and ruffled the dog's ears with one hand, holding the roses in his other hand.

"Where's Lily?" he asked the dog.

As if in response, Beans trotted back around the house. Nate followed, hearing the sounds of a shovel digging through dirt. For several moments, he stood beneath the branches of a plum tree and watched Lily turn soil in the garden. She wore a floppy hat, but her nose had sunburned anyway. And on her feet were a pair of blue, fuzzy slippers. He bit his tongue to keep from laughing at the endearing sight.

Tidy furrows lined the spacious area. Peas, lettuce and carrots had already started to sprout. She'd been busy since she arrived home eight weeks earlier and must have planted them within days of arriving in Jasper.

Tomato gates and a wheelbarrow filled with steer manure sat nearby. He eyed the wheelbarrow, wondering if she'd filled it and pushed it over here from the barn. It looked too heavy for her to push in her condition.

He frowned, glancing at her rounded stomach. Unable to explain the unreasonable amount of worry that filled his mind every time he saw her working so hard.

Dressed in blue jeans, Lily tucked a tendril of long, dark hair up into the hat. Time seemed to stand still while Nate gazed at her profile. Heavy curls of hair pooled around her shoulders. In the bright sunlight, her face gleamed with an ethereal glow. He remembered the soulful beauty of her eyes. The guarded expression while she'd sat quietly listening in church last week. The way her nose crinkled when she was troubled about something, which was most of the time.

She looked absolutely stunning in her dirty work clothes. If only she'd trust him. If only she could love him as much as he loved her.

His gaze lowered to her pregnancy, outlined by a too-tight man's T-shirt. Even though the short sleeves gaped from her thin arms and hung almost to her elbows, the cotton fabric gripped her midriff like a second skin.

The baby was growing. Ready to be born soon. And he wanted to be that child's father.

With the shovel, Lily took a scoop of manure, tossed it into a shallow hole she'd dug, mixed it well with the dirt, and then reached for a seedling tomato plant. The shovel caught in the soil and she stumbled.

Nate dropped the roses at the edge of the garden. In three long strides, he reached Lily's side and steadied her. She cried out in surprise, tilting her face up to gaze at him with wide, startled eyes.

"Nate! I didn't know you were here."

"Are you okay?" He caught the sweet scent of her shampoo and breathed in deeply.

She took a step back, forcing him to disengage his hands from around her arms. For just a moment, he'd forgotten that she didn't like to be touched.

"Yes, I'm fine. Just very clumsy these days."

She glanced at her tummy and he smiled at the wistful look in her eyes. There was something special about a pregnant woman. As if they held all the secrets to the universe within their soul. And he supposed that was true. The creation of a child worked hand-in-hand with God to bring a new spirit to earth. No wonder Nate couldn't take his eyes off this woman.

Realizing he was staring, he blinked and stepped over to retrieve the roses. He handed them to her, thinking how his attempt at gallantly courting her today had been a bit undone.

"These are for you."

The green tissue paper rustled as she took them, then gave him an impish smile. "I thought they were for my father."

He chuckled, enjoying her small attempt at humor. The wry smile softening her lips emboldened him. "I only give roses to a beautiful woman."

Furrows of confusion crinkled her brow. "They're lovely, but what are they for?"

He cleared his throat, feeling suddenly reticent and out-of-place. "Just because. Every woman ought to get flowers now and then."

She handed them back to him, her deep sigh signaling her frustration. "I can't accept them, Nate."

He refused to take them, putting his hands in his pants pockets instead. He glanced down at her slippers. "Are you starting a new shoe style?"

She chuckled. "My feet are swelling. I know working in my slippers will ruin them, but they're more comfortable than tight shoes."

"Sounds logical to me." In fact, her quirky behavior made him love her even more.

"You've been working long hours, Nate. I went out to feed the horses this morning and found it already done. You must have gotten up before dawn to drive all the way out here and take care of our chores before going into town to do your ranger work."

"It's no problem. Really," he said. And he meant it.

She blinked at his declaration. "But then you come out

again to work at night. Burning the candle at both ends so Dad and I won't overdue."

"It's just a labor of love."

She paused, as if considering his words. "But you look tired." She lifted a hand, as though she might caress his face. But then she lowered it again.

Oh, how he wished she'd touch him. How he wished she could open her heart and let him in. "I don't feel tired. In fact, I feel great now I've seen you today. Don't worry about me. You just take care of yourself and that baby."

He looked down at her as a ripple of movement crossed her tummy. His eyes widened. "Wow! Is that the baby moving?"

She nodded and pressed a hand to the top of her stomach. "She moves all the time. Lately, she's been doing tap dances on my rib cage. Sometimes she kicks so hard, she takes my breath away."

He stepped closer, hungering for just one touch. "I don't mean to embarrass you, but can I feel the baby move?"

Lily hesitated, then nodded. He lifted both hands and cupped her abdomen, surprised to find her stomach tight as a basketball. Standing so close, he could hear Lily breathing in shallow gasps, as though being this near to him unnerved her.

The baby wiggled, then jabbed Nate's palm with a tiny foot. Nate gasped and both he and Lily laughed. For several moments, Nate tracked the baby's movements lightly with his hands. Marveling at the miracle of life. Awed by the way this woman and her unborn child made him a better man inside and out.

Again and again, the baby kicked. And when Nate looked at Lily, he was surprised to find that they both had tears in their eyes.

"Lily," he whispered and kissed her forehead.

She looked up at him. So close. So lovely. Not pulling away. Not even flinching.

He lowered his head and kissed her lips. Soft, gentle and too quickly for his preference.

She stepped back, pushing against his chest. Her face flooded with color. "I...I better get back to work."

They'd shared something special in those few moments when he'd felt the baby move. Something extraordinary and wonderful. And yet, the barriers between them seemed even wider. In spite of everything, he couldn't help feeling that this baby belonged to him. His child. His woman.

The love of his life.

"Yeah, me, too. Thanks for letting me feel the baby. I can't tell you what it meant to me."

He stepped away, reluctant to leave her. Then he remembered something he dreaded talking with her about. "I was up in the chopper yesterday evening and I'm sorry to have to warn you of this. There's a huge debris torrent building above Emerald Ranch. At least fifty feet high."

Lily sucked back a harsh breath. "Have you told Dad?"

He shook his head. "I'll speak with him in a few minutes, but I wanted to tell you first. To see if you can convince him to move you and your horses to higher ground."

"I'll try, but he's as bullheaded as Bill Stokely."

"That was before he saw what happened at the Stokelys' place. Maybe now he'll believe me and move you out of here. It's just for a few weeks, until the danger passes."

She looked up at the mountain, her eyes filled with dread. "How long do we have?"

"There's no telling. Just get out of here as soon as possible. If you need help moving, I can do it for you." He jutted his chin toward the garden, trying to mask his own fear with light banter. "Looks like you're gonna have a lot of fresh vegetables to eat soon."

She held the bunch of roses to her chest and her sudden smile softened her face with an iridescent light. "Yes. My mother used to bottle peaches, pears, corn, string beans, tomatoes and anything else she could get her hands on. I used to help, so I think I can do it now."

He liked her willingness to try new things. "As long as it's not asparagus, I'm sure your dad will like that."

"Speaking of Dad, this morning we were discussing a plan to sell our horses. You've almost got Misty and Toots ready for buyers and I'd like to get your ideas on how we can market our new performance horse business."

He paused, thinking. Could asking her out really be this easy? Maybe the Lord had helped her play right into his hands. Nate had sure made this a matter of prayer often enough. He could use a little assistance wooing this woman. "Tell you what. I've got to go up on the mountain again tomorrow afternoon, after I've worked with the horses in the morning."

Her shoulders stiffened. "I don't think I can fly anymore. I'm too far along, Nate."

"No worries. I'll be driving up in my truck. It's just a few miles and I'll ensure you don't get bumped around on the dirt roads too much. My men are building new restrooms at one of the campgrounds and I want to check their work."

"Nate, remember I'm not interested in romance."

Okay, he'd planned for this reaction with a good, reasoning comeback. He'd actually practiced his response in front of the bathroom mirror this morning. Now he couldn't remember a word of it. His thoughts scattered with the gentle evening breeze blowing down from the Ruby Mountains. He only knew what he felt. Determined, yet bewildered. But he couldn't give up.

"Okay, then. No date. Just take a ride with me. It might be good for you to get away for a while. You need a break from work."

"So, it isn't a date?" Her brown eyes narrowed with suspicion.

He tried not to sound too eager. Hoping and praying she'd be amenable to his proposal. Unwilling to lie to her about anything ever. "I promise if you go with me, there'll be no proposals."

She folded her arms on top of her baby bump, looking so fragile. So careworn. "Okay. I really do want to go, but it's got to be by my rules. It's just an outing to check the new potties. No romance, no rings, no proposals. Just talk about buyers for our horses. Agreed?"

"Until I can convince you otherwise."

She shook her head. "Well, you can't."

Yet. He'd find a way to change her mind. "We'll leave from here at noon. Wear comfortable clothes and a good pair of walking shoes. If you have to wear the slippers, that's okay. I'll carry you."

She laughed and glanced at her stomach. "I don't think slippers will be necessary, but I can't go hiking, Nate."

"We won't. Don't worry. I'll take good care of you, but I don't want you to turn an ankle on the uneven ground we'll be walking on."

"Okay." She sounded doubtful but willing.

He hesitated. "And you should know something about me."

"What's that?" she asked.

"I don't let girls kiss me on a first date, even if it's not a real date."

She chuckled. "Now you're really scaring me."

He could tell from the twinkle in her eyes that she wasn't frightened one bit. And he almost gave a shout of victory. Because as small as it seemed, she had let him get close enough to kiss her and she had just teased him back. A major step in the right direction.

He paused. "Remember something. It's always darkest

before the dawn. So if you're going to steal your neighbor's newspaper, that's the best time to do it."

She cocked her head, looking confused. "They don't deliver the paper out here in the valley. And why would I want to steal my neighbor's newspaper anyway?"

"You wouldn't. I'm just keeping my promise to make you laugh as often as possible. You're not gonna let me down are you?"

She laughed, the sound low and sweet. "You're crazy, did you know that?"

"I'm crazy about you, babe. And did you know you're beautiful when you smile?"

She opened her mouth to say something, but he didn't give her the chance. She might change her mind about going up on the mountain with him. Instead, he gestured to the fields. "I'm gonna go help your dad now. I think we can get some hay harvested tonight and I'll still have time to work with two of the horses. If you need anything, just come to the edge of the fence and wave your arms. I'll see you and come running."

He turned and sauntered off, his heart bursting with joy. Tomorrow, he'd get to have her to himself. It didn't matter that he couldn't talk about romance. He'd get to spend time with Lily. Talk. Laugh. Learn more about her.

And maybe she'd start to care for him as much as he cared for her.

Chapter Eighteen

This was a big mistake. Lily knew it the moment she saw Nate walk to the stable with the horse he'd been riding that morning. She'd watched him working in the paddock, admiring his easy grace as his tall body rocked with the horse's stride. Rather than a separate entity, Nate seemed like a part of the horse. So comfortable in the saddle. So self-assured.

Toots was no longer over-rotating her right side. She held her head nice and low for cattle work and responded to the merest touch of Nate's heels. Under his gentle tutelage, she'd become a good cattle horse.

Now, Lily stood at the kitchen window peeling carrots for supper. Nate led the horse toward the stable. The filly pranced and waved her head before nudging Nate's arm with her nose. No doubt looking for another molasses treat. Thankfully Nate used discretion and never overdid it. He seemed to have an uncanny knack for knowing how much was too much so he didn't give the horses colic.

Nate disappeared into the stable. She knew he'd rub down the horse, making sure Toots was dry and had plenty of water. He babied each and every animal, soothing them. Teaching them that they could trust him.

Gentling them the way he was gentling her.

Lily shook her head, bolting the door on that thought. To save her life, she couldn't deny her excitement at going with him up on the mountain. She tried to ignore the tingling in the pit of her stomach, but it did little good. Somehow, Nate had wormed his way into her heart. She really liked this man. And that scared her beyond belief.

"He's sure good with the horses." Dad spoke from behind her.

"Yep." She couldn't bring herself to say anything more as Dad stood beside her. Instead, she reached for a towel to dry her hands.

"I knew he was the right man for the job. I just wish he had more time to spend here at the ranch with us."

It seemed they all had that sentiment, including Lily. She didn't want Nate here, yet when he was gone, she missed him horribly. Against her better judgment, he was growing on her. She just could not make sense of her jumbled emotions.

"Nate says he's taking you on a date this afternoon."

Lily huffed. "It's not a date. We're just going to spend some time together."

Dad reached for a chunk of carrot and popped it into his mouth to chew. "That's a date, darlin'. And it's okay by me. I figure it's about time you found yourself a decent man you can depend on."

She ignored that remark. "Have you thought anymore about the debris jam he saw building up above the ranch?"

"Yep."

"And?"

"And I'm not going anywhere."

She turned. "Dad, I saw the dam above the Stokelys' ranch. It was small in comparison to what Nate says is sitting above us. He says it could take out our entire ranch."

"Ah, don't worry, darlin'. Nothing's ever happened to the ranch before and it won't happen now."

"But it happened to the Stokelys! It could be worse for us."

"The Stokelys' ranch sits close to the mountain, but ours doesn't. No flood can come down the mountain and reach our house."

"Nate says it could. He said the force of the water and the width of the debris can be that strong."

"Then leave if you want to," he yelled.

Lily flinched and felt the blood drain from her face. "I want you to go with me, Daddy. We'll take the horses and move them to higher ground, just for a few weeks until the danger has passed."

His face reddened with anger. "I said I'm not leaving. Don't ask me again. You do what you want."

He reached for an old newspaper he'd read a zillion times and sat down in his recliner. With a whack of the paper, he opened it and scanned it with his gaze, ignoring her.

It didn't help matters when Nate came from the barn packing a large basket. He must have made it himself and put it in the shade of the barn to protect it from the summer heat. She'd planned for a drive up the mountain, not a picnic lunch.

He opened the door to his truck and slid the basket onto the backseat. Then, he glanced at one of the side mirrors and smoothed his damp hair. He must have washed up in the stable.

Getting ready for their date—which wasn't really a date.

Lily sighed. Why pretend? It was a date, any way she looked at it. There were so many facets to this man and she couldn't help being intrigued by him.

He had no idea what he was getting himself into by being around her. He didn't have children, so he couldn't know all the work involved in raising a baby. Especially a baby he hadn't fathered. Diapers, late-night feedings and lots of bills. Lily couldn't dump all of that on Nate. Unless she was absolutely certain he could take it for keeps.

As he walked toward the house to get her, a swarm of butterflies settled in her stomach. Dressed in blue jeans that shaped his lean legs, he walked with a confident stride. Obviously he wasn't nervous about their date...er, outing.

Going with Nate would just give him a false sense of hope. She'd warned him she didn't want a romantic involvement. And she meant it. If he got hurt, it was his own fault.

Wasn't it?

His knock sounded on the front door. As she walked through the living room, she decided she'd tell him she couldn't go. She wasn't feeling well. She'd use the baby as an excuse to stay home.

Opening the door, she found him smiling in anticipation. With all the time he'd spent working outside in the sunshine, his face and arms had turned a golden hue. His brown eyes crinkled as he looked at her from head to toe.

"You look beautiful, Lily."

She could almost say the same about him. Her insides melted like butter smoothed over a hot piece of cornbread. "Thank you."

She stepped back and he followed her inside. His slightly damp hair curled at the nape of his neck and she resisted the urge to reach up and thread her fingers through it.

"If at first you don't succeed, then skydiving is not for you."

"What?"

He repeated the question, smiling expectantly.

"Oh, no. Not another silly joke." She laughed in spite of herself. Not because it was funny, but because he was trying so hard. He made her feel special. Like she meant something to him.

"No one's ever tried to make me happy before," she confided.

"You don't like my jokes?"

She covered her mouth with one hand, trying hard not to

giggle like a teenage girl. What was it about this man that made her feel so flighty and joyful? "Well, your jokes are kind of lame. Did you think them up yourself?"

"Nah, I got them off the internet." He waved a hand in the air. "Guess I need a new source, huh?"

"Something like that."

He stepped nearer. "You deserve to be happy, but I think you're afraid. I can't blame you, Lily. Not after what you've been through. But think about it. Is this really how you want to live the next fifty years of your life? Alone. No one to love, just so you won't get hurt again?"

His candor left her breathless and exposed. How did he know so much about her? Her first reaction was to get angry. But as she gazed up into his eyes, all she saw there was an honest desire to help.

"Nate, please don't."

He stepped back. "If you ever change your mind, please let me know. I don't want to wait any longer than necessary."

But she wouldn't. Loving this man would cost her too much.

"I...I'll just get my jacket and be ready to go." As she reached into the coat closet, her mind whirled with a dozen arguments why she shouldn't love him. Why she couldn't accept his marriage proposal and just fold herself into his arms.

Outside, he opened the truck door for her and helped her climb up. Sitting back in her seat, she decided to relax and enjoy the ride. But her body thrummed with excitement and she couldn't explain the light, carefree feeling in her chest. The first she'd had in years.

"Does your dad need help moving the horses to higher ground?" Nate glanced at Lily as he drove them over the dirt road leading up the campground at Barton's Peak. She looked beautiful with sunlight glinting off her russet hair, showing highlights of red and gold.

"No, he says he's not going anywhere."

"What?"

"He's acting like an ostrich with its head in the sand. He doesn't think we'll end up like the Stokelys."

Nate snorted. "Then you need to go into town without him. Would Clara let you stay at her house for a while?"

"Yes, but I won't leave Dad."

"Ah, come on. Be reasonable. Your dad's a grown man, but you're pregnant. You need to be where you and the baby will be safe."

"I won't leave him," she said again.

Nate grit his teeth, showing an irritated tick along his lean jaw. For just a fraction of a moment, Lily expected him to explode at her. That's what Tommy would have done. But she'd learned that wasn't Nate's way. He didn't like what she'd said, but he'd never hurt her. She knew that now.

She trusted him.

True to his word, Nate didn't discuss romance and he made Lily laugh at least a dozen times. She gave a shout of joy when he informed her that he had a buyer set up for six of their horses.

"You're kidding. Who is it?"

"A rancher I know in Elko. He's got four sons, all of who participate in rodeo. They saw the exhibition with Toots and Peg and he's anxious to buy our horses."

Nate told her the offered price and she laughed with relief. "That's more than fair. Oh, Nate, I don't know how to thank you enough."

"No need to thank me, Lily. We're in this venture together, remember?"

Yes, together. She thoroughly enjoyed the afternoon. After Nate inspected the new restrooms and surveyed the repairs to the campground, he spread out their lunch on a blanket beneath a tall aspen. Turkey and Swiss cheese sandwiches, grapes, potato chips and chocolate chip cookies. By the time he dropped her off back at home, Lily almost wished she hadn't put him under promise not to talk about romance. The front porch light showed the way as he walked her to the door. He squeezed her hand and gazed down into her eyes. For just a moment, she thought he might kiss her again. And a part of her wished he would. She admitted only to herself that she no longer felt afraid.

"Thank you for a wonderful day. Good night." He stepped away, waiting until she went inside.

Dad must have gone to bed already, leaving a lamp on in the living room for her. As she watched through the living room window while the headlights of Nate's truck pulled away, she realized she'd almost forgotten the danger the ranch faced. She'd almost forgotten her vow to never get close to Nate.

Late that night, Lily tossed and turned, too worried to sleep. At almost eight months pregnant, she just could not get comfortable no matter what position she tried. The baby had wedged a foot in Lily's rib cage and the powerful kicks made her gasp.

The thought of being stuck here inside the house during a debris torrent filled Lily with utter terror. What if she fell and injured the baby? She was too big to flee from a flood.

She tried to sleep, but an inner voice kept warning her to get up and act now. Before it was too late.

What should she do?

Sitting up in bed, she tossed the covers aside and swung her feet to the carpeted floor. Drawing back the lacy curtains at her window, she gazed out at the darkness. No stars or moon in sight. Heavy clouds must be blanketing the sky. Down the hall, she heard Dad's deep snores coming from his bedroom.

And then she got a crazy idea. Crazy but practical. And necessary. If Dad wouldn't take action, then she would.

If she moved the horses to higher ground herself, Dad would have no choice but to accept it. It'd be done. He might get angry, but the horses would be safe.

She dressed and slipped out of the house as quietly as possible. Down by the barn, she ensured one of the four-wheelers was filled with gas. Next to Misty's stall, she paused for a moment and pressed the palm of her hand against her distended stomach.

"Okay, baby, we've got a lot of work to do. You just rest and be quiet and Mommy will take care of everything."

It was one of the rare occasions when she spoke out loud to her child. Allowing herself this precious luxury gave her added strength to do what lay ahead. She'd move slow and careful, not overdoing or straining herself. But she'd be tired by morning.

Breathing deep the crisp night air, she caught the fragrant aroma of honeysuckle and sage. The scent of rain higher up in the mountains.

The breeze cooled her heated face and arms. She tossed a warm jacket onto the back of the four-wheeler just in case, but doubted she'd need it.

Moving with precision, Lily haltered each of their yearlings and the older horses, tying them in a long string. When possible, she placed a gate or barrel between herself and the horses, to protect her stomach in case one of the animals bumped against her.

The new colts and fillies would follow their mommas without coercion. Some of the younger animals hadn't been trained to lead this way. It'd be a long night if she had to take them each individually to the higher pasture and she prayed they'd be too tired to resist.

She led the animals east, toward their pasture near Watt's

Mountain three miles away. Beans trotted beside her, giving her some small comfort. She couldn't help wishing Nate were here with her now. She'd come to depend on him. To trust him.

To care for him deeply.

No, she couldn't think about her feelings now. She had to concentrate. To focus on the dark road ahead.

Peering through the black shadows, she moved the horses at a slow walk. Pegasus stood in the corral closest to the barn, his beautifully shaped head up high, nostrils flared, ears pricked forward, his eyes glinting with intelligence as he watched them go. He pranced back and forth, snorting and pawing the dirt. He didn't like being left behind.

Lily shook her head. "No, boy. You can't come with us this trip. I'll be back for you in a little while."

She turned her attention back to the mares and colts. A quarter of a mile up the road, she finally turned on the headlights. It'd be catastrophic if one of the horses stepped in a hole and went down. Better to take this journey with deliberate and safe caution than to be sorry later on. She also didn't want the lights to wake up Dad.

The four-wheeler's motor made a low humming sound. Lily steered the quad with both hands, holding on tight as she tackled the bumpy dirt road. She glanced over her shoulder now and then, to ensure the horses were moving okay. When she saw their heads down as they plodded along, her chest swelled with relief.

Thank you, Lord. Thank You for being with me tonight.

She carried the prayer in her heart, thanking God for all her many blessings. And right there, in the middle of the night, with nothing but darkness and horses as her companions, she realized God had forgiven her. A calming peace enveloped her, like the warmth of a new summer day, except it filled her heart and mind. God had her life in His hands and He wouldn't let anything bad happen to her as long as she had faith in Him. This was where she belonged. She could stop running now.

She was home. Really home.

She'd felt so alone for so long. But no more. She realized with brutal force that she'd been pushing away the very people who were trying to be there for her. Dad, Nate and even her unborn baby. She didn't know what life would bring to her, but she knew she could face anything as long as she had God and her family beside her.

Her family.

With serene clarity, she realized that included Nate. She couldn't imagine life without him. They belonged together and she could hardly wait to tell him so.

Minutes ticked by, her heart pounding. A misting rain started falling and Lily shivered. She stopped the quad long enough to thrust her arms through the sleeves of the jacket she'd brought along. The horses shifted nervously. Tendrils of damp hair fell into her eyes and she brushed them back impatiently. Why did it have to rain just now?

Back on her way, she blinked, her eyelashes spiked with rain. She grit her teeth hard to keep them from chattering. Her fingers felt like blocks of ice. Flexing them around the handgrips didn't help much. She should have worn gloves.

Throughout this activity, she noticed the baby didn't move much. Probably too cramped with Lily bent over to drive the four-wheeler.

And then she started having doubts.

What was she thinking? Out here in a rainstorm in the middle of the night at almost eight months pregnant. If there wasn't so much at stake, she'd have stayed home in her warm bed. But as it stood, she wasn't willing to take a chance with their livestock. She'd be home soon and then she could rest.

The baby would be okay. She'd be okay. The Lord would bless her. She must have faith.

The headlights reflected off the wide metal gate just ahead and she breathed a sigh of relief. She'd made it. Now she just needed to put the horses inside the paddock and go retrieve Peg.

She glanced at the sky, finding not a single star to light her way. She couldn't read the time on her wrist watch, but figured she had just enough time to bring Peg here and get back home before sunrise.

And her inevitable confrontation with Dad.

They'd rarely used the east pasture because it had no water source. Nothing but scrubby grass and jackrabbits grew here. Dad had always talked about piping water in but had never gotten around to it. First thing in the morning, she'd fill a tank with water and use a tractor to drive it over for the horses to drink. She could bring in several bales of hay, too. It wouldn't hurt to feed and house the animals in the pasture for a couple of weeks until Nate told them they were out of danger. Then they could move the horses back home. By the time Dad awakened in the morning, the deed would be done and he'd have to accept her decision.

Of course, Dad could always move the horses back to the ranch, but Lily figured he'd let it go at that point. This was important and Lily wouldn't take chances with their livelihood. Then she'd work on getting Dad to move into town with her for a short time. She'd called Clara before going on her date with Nate. Clara had a spare bedroom for Dad and Lily didn't mind sleeping on the couch as long as she had lots of pillows to support her back.

It was the right thing to do. Lily just hoped her stamina held out until she could go and retrieve Peg.

Chapter Nineteen

The wipers thwacked across the windshield, sluicing off great droplets of rain as Nate drove toward Emerald Ranch. Before he'd gone to bed, he'd studied the thick, gray clouds blanketing the sky and worried about the potential of more flooding.

Especially above Emerald Ranch. It wouldn't take much to push the debris dam down on top of Lily and her father.

And so Nate hadn't slept at all. He'd laid down several times and closed his eyes, but anxiousness kept him so agitated that he couldn't rest. A persistent, inner voice kept warning him to get up and drive out to the ranch. To check on the Hansens and see that they were safe.

The headlights of Nate's truck gleamed off the wet asphalt, which soon gave way to gravel and then muddy potholes. The tires bounced hard across the ruts, but Nate refused to slow his speed. Tall mercury lights glimmered from the yards of each ranch house as he passed through the valley. A faint spray of dawn sunlight gleamed just above the Ruby Mountains, dimmed by charcoal clouds hovering overhead. He couldn't explain the urgency building within him. He only knew that he had to make certain Lily was okay. Had to see her right now!

When Emerald Ranch came into view, the clock on the

dashboard showed 5:18 a.m. As if on cue, the rain abated to a gentle sprinkling. As he pulled into the front driveway, Nate stared toward the barn. Lily stood beside a four-wheeler, soaking wet in a pair of blue jeans and cowboy boots. Hank paced back and forth, gesturing wildly and shouting. They didn't even look his way, seeming not to notice they had an early morning visitor.

What was going on?

Peg stood not far away from the barn, his glistening coat steaming in the warming sunlight. Only the horse seemed to notice Nate's presence, turning his proud head and blowing from his nostrils as he stomped one hoof.

Nate killed the motor and stepped out of the truck. The tall mercury lights by the corrals and stable illuminated Hank's angry face. His furious voice filled the crisp, morning air. From the pallid expression on Lily's face, this couldn't be good. She'd wrapped her arms around her baby stomach, her thick ponytail lying like a sodden dishcloth over her right shoulder. Tendrils of hair clung to her pale cheeks, her eyes red from crying.

As he walked over to them, Nate saw a shiver course over Lily's body, like a giant wave across the ocean. Nate's protective instincts kicked into overdrive. He didn't know what was going on, but she was wet and cold and he wanted her warm and safe.

"Can't believe you did this." Hank paced back and forth in front of his daughter, his hands clenched, his back rigid. "You could have injured one of the horses or hurt yourself. You could have hurt my grandbaby. What possessed you, girl? What were you thinking?"

Lily looked past her father at Nate and in the depths of her brown eyes, he saw a desperation he hadn't seen there before. Fear, disappointment and pain.

"Lil, are you okay?" Nate brushed past Hank, not even caring that he surprised the older man.

"Nate! You're really here. I prayed that you'd come and here you are." Her words sounded like a whispered plea. Tears of relief ran down her cheeks.

"What are you doing here, Nate?" Hank whirled about and stared, a moment of surprise breaking through the red haze of rage covering his face.

"I came to make sure Lil was okay. I kept worrying about her and couldn't sleep." Without asking permission, Nate whipped his jacket off and wrapped it around Lily's shoulders. Then he rubbed her arms to get her warm. She didn't fight him but leaned close, her breath rushing against the open collar of his shirt. She felt small and fragile and he wouldn't let her go until he was certain she was all right.

"You're freezing cold," he murmured against her hair.

"I…I am cold." Her teeth chattered and she hugged her round abdomen.

"What happened?" His question was for her alone, but Hank interrupted their private moment.

"Can you believe this?" Hank bellowed. "She's been up all night in a rainstorm, moving our horses to the east pasture. I told her not to do it, but would she listen to me? No sirree. I'm just her father after all. I don't know anything. When in all her life has she ever listened to me?"

"I did what I thought was right," she spoke against Nate's shirt, a wobbly murmur that sounded dangerously near to tears. "I…I wanted to protect us. I think the ranch is in danger. I trust you, Nate, so I moved the horses. I can't believe I did it by myself, but I never felt alone. The Lord was with me. Every step of the way."

She spoke so softly that he almost didn't hear. Her confession tore at his heart. How he wished he'd been here for her.

"I'm glad to hear that, sweetheart, but now I think you need to rest."

She clung to him, her voice low and urgent. "But I have so much I want to tell you, Nate. I had a special experience out there alone in the dark. I feel so free. So forgiven."

Was she hysterical and babbling? He wasn't sure. Obviously she'd had a spiritual experience tonight. The fact that she wanted to share it with Nate touched his heart deeply.

"I'm glad, Lil. So glad. But I'm worried about you. Let me take you inside now."

She pulled away, looking up at his face. "But I still need to get Peg out of here. The quad got stuck in the mud. I couldn't get back in time before Dad caught me. Please help me get Peg out of here."

Nate's heart gave a powerful squeeze. He couldn't ignore her plea. He looked down into her eyes and saw the supplication on her face. The helpless, wilted expression of a woman who'd fought hard, but needed him to fight for her now.

"All you've done is create more work for us." Hank drew back his booted foot and kicked one of the muddy tires on the quad. "If you'd listened to me just once in your life, you wouldn't be in this mess. But no! You had to run off and do what you wanted."

The conversation had shifted. Somehow Nate didn't believe this was about moving the horses anymore, but rather about Lily leaving home when she was young and ending up pregnant.

"Now isn't the time to discuss this," Nate spoke to Hank. "We need to get Lil inside where she can lie down."

Lily glanced toward the corral where Peg pranced back and forth, neck arched, tail high in the air. No doubt the normally docile stallion sensed trouble and didn't like it. With Hank's raised voice, the horse had become agitated.

"You left Peg outside all night in the rain. What if he gets sick because of what you've done? We'll lose everything," Hank said.

Lily cringed, looking as though her father had just socked her in the nose. Tears slipped down her cheeks. Nate brushed them away.

"I'm sorry, Daddy."

"Sorry won't make this right," Hank growled.

"Stop it, Hank. You've said enough," Nate admonished. He knew he had no right to interfere, but he wasn't about to stand by and let Hank verbally abuse Lily.

Hank didn't say another word, but he blustered and fumed, his face red as a charging bull.

Feeling the trembling in Lily's body ease to a slow ripple, Nate stepped back and took her arm, prepared to lead her to the house. She bent slightly at the waist. Her stomach tightened, her face contorted in pain.

"Are you okay, Lil?"

She shook her head.

"Is it the baby?"

He could see the answer in her eyes. She didn't feel well. She tossed another fleeting look toward Peg, her gaze filled with apprehension. "We've got to get Peg out of here."

"Are you in pain? Or just cold and worn out?" Nate held her arm.

"I...I think I'm having contractions." She rested a thin hand against the side of her stomach and let out a low groan.

Oh, boy! Not what Nate wanted to hear right now.

"You're having the baby now?" Hank's angry voice changed to stunned amazement.

"I think I'm in labor," Lily said.

"But it's too early." Hank's eyes creased with concern. For all his bad temper, he still cared about his daughter. Very much.

"Okay, we can handle this. Let's get you into my truck and

we'll drive you into town and…" Nate didn't get the chance to finish his spoken thoughts. A low rumbling filled the air, like thunder on the mountain.

They all turned toward the west, but the looming barn and stable stood in the way and they couldn't see anything unusual. The sound escalated until it filled their ears. Like the rushing of a massive freight train. A deep, frenzied giant with the strength to crush them all.

Headed straight toward them.

Prickles of alarm dotted Nate's flesh. He'd never witnessed this before, but people had described it to him.

The stable groaned and swayed, as though it were a living being. The splintering of lumber filled the air.

No, not now. It couldn't be.

"Hank, get her in my truck and get out of here." Nate tossed his keys to Hank before thrusting Lily into her father's arms.

"What is it? What's wrong?" Hank asked, looking confused.

"No time to explain. Just go!" Nate ordered as he turned toward the corral.

Lily gasped. "Peg!"

Hank just stood there. "Nate, what are you—"

"Go!" he roared.

Finally Hank moved into action, clasping Lily's arm. Tugging her toward Nate's truck.

"Nate! Come with us. Please," Lily called over her shoulder.

Nate didn't respond. He had only moments to act or it'd be too late.

Thank heaven Hank didn't argue any further. He wrapped an arm around Lily's shoulders and ran with her to Nate's truck. Beans barked and followed them at a sprint, jumping inside the truck with Lily just before Hank slammed the door.

Nate sprinted toward the corral. He couldn't let Lily down.

She was depending on him. So was Hank. If Nate hurried, he might just make it. Before they lost the stallion. Before they lost everything.

Including his own life.

Lily gripped the arm rest on the truck door as Dad hopped into the driver's seat, turned the key and put the vehicle in gear. The tires spun gravel as the truck zoomed forward, racing toward the main road.

Swiveling in her seat, Lily stared out the back window. Even from this distance, she could hear the horrible crash as the roof of the stable fell in on itself. A mountain of tree trunks, boulders the size of compact cars and sludge rolled over the top of it, a wall of debris over twenty-feet high. The torrent flattened the stable within seconds, the mound of mud gaining momentum as it picked up more debris and undulated across the yard. The mess surrounded the barn like a giant mote of mud.

Nate had been right. The dam had finally broken loose with a vengeance. The debris torrent consumed everything in its path.

Nate! He'd die if he stayed there.

Her gaze scanned the corrals. She bit back a sob when she spied him. He stood on the top rung of the fence. He launched himself toward Peg, landing on the stallion's back, clutching handfuls of mane. Peg screamed and reared, pawing the air with his front hooves. Nate tightened his legs around the animal's sides, clinging to its back. When the stud lowered his front hooves to the ground, Nate kicked his boot heels against the horse's flanks.

The stallion gave a shrill whinny and ran toward the opposite side of the corral. No, they wouldn't make it. Peg wasn't a jumper. He'd never been trained for such a stunt. They'd crash into the rails, breaking Nate's neck and Peg's legs.

Lily couldn't move. Couldn't breathe. They wouldn't clear the fence. Both horse and rider could be killed—

The horse sailed over the top rail with Nate lying low across his back. The stallion seemed to fly, reminding Lily of a winged Pegasus. She'd never seen such a beautiful, blessed sight in all her life.

As one body, the horse and rider landed safely on the other side. The stallion didn't pause but kept moving. His sturdy body bunched, strong muscles pumping, galloping to safety as he raced across the grassy fields.

Like a giant wave in the ocean, the mountain of mud trailed after Nate and Peg. Nipping at the horse's heels.

Chasing them.

Lily watched in horror as the quad, the tractor and even the tool shed disappeared in a melee of sludge. The debris torrent moved as fast as a sprinting horse, swallowing everything within its path. If Peg hadn't had a head start, the horse would have been swallowed up in the mud.

And then the torrent spread out across the paddock and corrals surrounding the barn, finally losing momentum. Coating every available surface.

Lily could contain her emotions no longer. Sobs trembled over her body. It took several moments for her to realize Dad had stopped the truck at the top of the hill and held her in his arms.

"There, darlin'. Don't cry now. We're gonna be all right."

"Daddy, I…I'm so sorry."

"No, darlin'. I'm the one who's sorry. I should have listened to you. I should have listened to Nate. I'll never make that mistake again."

"Oh, Dad." She hugged him tight.

"You've become a wonderful woman and I'm ashamed for ever doubting you," he said. "We would have lost all our horses if you hadn't disobeyed me. I love you so much. You're wiser than I am. If I ever lost you, I don't know what I'd do. Will you forgive a doddering old fool? I'm so sorry, darlin'. Please forgive me."

Finally. Finally the words she'd longed to hear. "I love you, too, Dad. More than I can ever say. I'm sorry, too. For everything."

She spoke through her tears, knowing she might not share this mushy stuff with her father again for years, if ever. But it didn't matter. They both knew how they felt about one another and she could accept that. It was enough.

Minutes later, Nate joined them, walking Peg to let the horse cool down. Dad rolled down the window of his truck so they could talk.

"She okay?" Nate called as he dismounted.

"No, I'm not," Lily spoke before Dad could respond.

Both men stared at her, their eyebrows lifted in alarm.

"Nate, Dad's gonna take me into town. Can you take Peg over to the Stokelys' place and leave him there?" she asked. "See if Bill will drive you into town to meet us at the clinic. I've never had a baby before, but I'm almost certain I've gone into labor. And I'm not due for five more weeks."

Nate nodded, his expression stoic and rather nervous. If Lily hadn't been feeling so rotten, she would have laughed at the way the two men hurried to meet her request.

And that's when Lily realized how much she loved them both. How much she never wanted to be parted from Dad or Nate ever again. Come what may.

It hadn't been easy, this forgiveness thing. But God had performed a miracle in her life. He'd brought her home. He'd kept her safe. He'd given her a family to cherish.

Now she just needed to tell Nate how she felt about him. And pray that he'd forgive her stubborn foolishness for ever pushing him away.

* * *

Hours later, Lily released a sigh of relief. Her contractions had stopped and the doctor told her the baby should be okay.

"But don't push it, Lily. It's bed rest for you until your due date. No more all-nighters in a rainstorm with your horses. No more housework. No more cooking and gardening. No more anything except taking care of your own needs. Or I'll put you in a hospital bed for the next five weeks. Understand?" Dr. Kenner gave her a scolding frown.

Lily nodded, not daring to argue. Somehow, she'd figure out a way to take care of the horses. The Lord would help her. He always had. She just needed to have faith and He'd see her through.

"She'll behave. I'll make sure of that."

Lily looked up and found Nate leaning against the door-jamb, his thumbs slung through the sides of his belt buckle. His warm gaze rested on her, his eyes narrowed with gentle determination.

"Nate! I'm so glad you're here."

"You are?"

"Oh, yes!" She didn't even try to fight the glittery feeling she had inside. Not when he was the one person she longed to see more than any other.

"I'll leave her in your hands, then." As the doctor left the room, Lily sat up, moving her left arm carefully so she didn't pull out the IV.

"Are you really happy to see me?" Nate rested his hands by his sides as he sauntered forward and stood next to the bed.

"Oh, yes. So very happy." She met his gaze, amazed by the welling of love that overflowed her heart. In such a short time, she'd learned that her capacity to love never ceased. Soon, she'd have a new baby to love. It just went on and on, growing with each new member of her family.

Nate's somber expression didn't soften as he jutted his chin toward her large stomach. "That little girl has been through an awful lot. Both of you have. This was a close call, Lil."

"I know. We could have lost the entire ranch instead of just the stable and some corrals. Thank goodness Dad and I updated our insurance policy right after the Stokelys' ranch was hit. Our policy includes flood coverage."

"I'm very glad, but that's not what I'm talking about."

She frowned and cocked her head. "What do you mean?"

His eyes narrowed. "You could have had the baby early. And I'd like us to be married before our baby comes."

She sucked back a surprised gasp and tried to swallow around the sudden lump in her throat. "Our baby?"

"Yes, ma'am." He glanced at her tummy. "I know I didn't father that little girl, but she's my child just the same. I want her to grow up knowing we both love her. I want her to grow up knowing me."

A spear of happiness pierced Lily's heart and she couldn't keep herself from smiling wide. "What exactly are you proposing?"

"I think you know." His tight mouth twitched with a barely concealed smile.

She gave a hoarse croak of laughter. "Yes, I know. But will you ask me one more time, please? Just so I can say yes?"

He lowered to one knee, his head and broad shoulders barely showing above the high hospital bed. She couldn't see when his hand slipped inside his pants pocket, but he produced her mother's engagement ring and placed it on her finger before squeezing her hand tight.

"Marry me, Lillian Hansen. If I have to beg, I will. But I'd rather not have to ask you a third time. I love you. More than I can ever say. Please be mine forever."

His voice sounded insistent, persuasive even. And Lily tugged on his arm to get him to stand up and hug her. He obliged her with a minimum of confusion. As the warmth of his solid arms slid around her shoulders, she felt so comforted. So safe and wanted.

"Oh, yes, Nate. I'll gladly marry you," she whispered against his ear before kissing his lips. She gazed adoringly at his chiseled face, unable to see through the haze of tears filling her eyes. "Don't worry, dear. You won't have to ask me again. I've learned where I belong. I love you, too. So much. I've been such a dope to resist you. I should have seen what the Lord tried to show me again and again."

As he leaned over her, his wide smile of pleasure told her everything she needed to know. "And what's that, sweetheart?"

"That you're the man for me. And I'm the gal for you. It's that simple. I should have trusted you from the start. You saved my life. You and the Lord's love have made me whole again."

"I feel the same about you, Lil. I never knew how lonely I was until you came along. Being with you completes me." He lowered his head, his lips grazing hers in a soft kiss.

"Ahem!"

They broke apart, staring at the door where Dad stood hat in hand, looking beet red with embarrassment.

"I…I'm sorry to interrupt, but does this mean we're gonna have a wedding? Do we get to keep the baby?"

Nate glanced at Lily and waited for her confirmation. She answered loud and clear, her voice vibrating with contentment. "It sure does, Daddy. And the sooner we get married, the better. We want to make it legal before Rose is born."

"Rose?" Nate asked, his eyes aglow with love.

She nodded and bit her bottom lip. Her entire body quaked with joy. "Yes, after my mother."

He kissed her and she felt his chuckle rumbling deep in his chest. "How about Rose Allison?"

She lifted one brow. "Allison?"

"After my mother."

She said the name several times, trying it out on her tongue. "Rose Allison Coates. Yes, I think that name is absolutely perfect."

Hank's laughter filled the room and he slapped his scruffy cowboy hat against his thigh. "So do I, darlin'. So do I. I'm sure glad you're finally getting hitched. Now Nate can stay out at the ranch all the time where he belongs."

"I'll still have to drive into town for my ranger job, but I can take care of the horses, too," Nate said.

Lily smiled. "As long as you come home to me each night, I don't care what you do for a living."

"You won't be able to keep me away," he promised her.

And with Hank's blessing, Lily married the man of her dreams later that week. Three weeks later, they welcomed little Rose into their home. A healthy, perfect baby girl.

"Our first child. Except for her mother, I've never seen anything so beautiful in all my life." Nate spoke in awe as he held the sleeping infant in his arms. His large finger looked so big and strong with Rose's small hand wrapped around it. He gazed at the child with an expression of utter rapture. His child.

Lily gave a playful grimace and pressed her hands against her abdomen. "It's hard to think about having another baby after the labor and delivery I just went through."

"Do you mind so much?" He leaned over to smile into her eyes and kiss her lips.

"Of course not. My mom used to say having a child was nine months of hardship for a lifetime of joy. Knowing what Daddy went through with me, I suspect it's a lifetime of hardship, too. But I'd gladly go through it again as long as our children are healthy, happy and love the Lord."

"I agree. We'll teach our children to trust in God and serve

Him." Nate kissed her again, very sweetly. His lopsided smile and the loving emotion gleaming in his eyes spoke volumes.

What more could Lily ask for? The Lord had given her everything. And so much more.

* * * * *

*Look for another wonderful book
from Leigh Bale in early 2013,
only from Love Inspired books!*

Dear Reader,

Have you ever made a serious mistake in your life? One that led you down a dark path that pulled you away from God and broke the hearts of your loved ones?

All of us sin. No one is perfect, except Jesus Christ, our Savior. Sin alienates us from God and deadens our spiritual soul. Because God knew we could not live a perfect life here in mortality, Christ came to rescue us from our wrongdoings. Justice demands restitution for our wrongs. But how can we, as imperfect beings, ever pay the price to make things right again? We cannot. We needed a mediator to atone for our sins. Otherwise we could not be forgiven. Christ paid that price for each of us.

In *The Forest Ranger's Child,* the heroine comes to the realization that Christ has atoned for her sins. He suffered excruciating physical and spiritual pain so that we all might be made whole. I am amazed by the love and great sacrifice my Savior has offered each and every one of us. All we need to do to take advantage of this great gift is repent and forsake our sins. What a perfect plan our Heavenly Father has given us. What a perfect love He offers all His children on earth.

I hope you enjoy reading *The Forest Ranger's Child,* and I invite you to visit my website at www.LeighBale.com to learn more about my books.

May you find peace in the Lord's words!
Leigh Bale

Questions for Discussion

1. Lily Hansen returns home after being gone for years, hoping to rebuild her relationship with her estranged father and the Lord. Pregnant and alone, she doesn't know where else to turn. Do you think she made the right decision by going home? What would you have done instead?

2. From their first meeting, Lily feels comfortable and safe in Nathan's presence. Have you ever connected with someone in this way? If so, who was it? Did this person feel the same way about you?

3. Hank Hansen is Lily's gruff father. Why do you think it is so hard for Hank to tell her he loves her? Do you have a problem telling your family members that you love them or showing them physical affection? Why or why not?

4. Knowing about Lily's past, why do you think she has a deep and abiding distrust of all men? Do you think she was right to be distrustful of Nathan, even after he had saved her life from the flash flood? Why or why not?

5. Nate was raised by a single mother who suffered guilt and isolation most of her adult life. For this reason, he has compassion for Lily's plight. Do you believe Lily deserved to be ostracized by people at church and within her community because of what she'd done? Why or why not?

6. Lily returns home seeking a safe haven where she can have her baby. But when she arrives, she discovers that her father is ailing and suffering from financial trouble.

This causes Lily to think more about her father's needs than her own. Do you think it was good for Lily to serve her father instead of dwelling on her own problems? Why or why not?

7. Lily is torn between keeping her unborn child and giving the baby up for adoption. Because of how she'd messed up her life, Lily doesn't believe she's the best mother for her child. If Lily hadn't found love and decided to marry Nate, what do you think she should have done with her baby? Why?

8. When Clara comes to visit, Lily compares her past mistakes with Clara's seeming success with career and family. Lily feels like a failure in comparison, yet she's determined to change her life for the better. Do you ever compare your life with others? Do you look for the good in your life, or the bad?

9. When Lily discovers her father is suffering from financial troubles, she is tempted to criticize him the way he has always done with her. Instead, she decides to sell her mother's ring so she can help. Why is it so tempting to criticize those people closest to us?

10. Because she fears criticism for being pregnant and unmarried, Lily is tempted to stay at her father's ranch, far away from other people. Do you think this is wise? Why or why not? How should Lily handle other people's disapproval?

11. When Lily discovers her father has a serious illness that could be terminal, she realizes she's taken him for

granted all her life. Do you have people you take for granted? How might you appreciate them more?

12. When Nate first proposes to Lily, she doesn't believe she loves him. He offers safety and security and a name for her unborn child. Do you think she should have agreed to marry him anyway? Why or why not?

INSPIRATIONAL

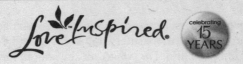

COMING NEXT MONTH
AVAILABLE JUNE 19, 2012

Look for these and other Love Inspired books wherever books are sold, including most bookstores, supermarkets, discount stores and drugstores.

LICNM0612

REQUEST YOUR FREE BOOKS!

2 FREE INSPIRATIONAL NOVELS
PLUS 2
FREE
MYSTERY GIFTS

YES! Please send me 2 FREE Love Inspired® novels and my 2 FREE mystery gifts (gifts are worth about $10). After receiving them, if I don't wish to receive any more books, I can return the shipping statement marked "cancel." If I don't cancel, I will receive 6 brand-new novels every month and be billed just $4.49 per book in the U.S. or $4.99 per book in Canada. That's a saving of at least 22% off the cover price. It's quite a bargain! Shipping and handling is just 50¢ per book in the U.S. and 75¢ per book in Canada.* I understand that accepting the 2 free books and gifts places me under no obligation to buy anything. I can always return a shipment and cancel at any time. Even if I never buy another book, the two free books and gifts are mine to keep forever.

105/305 IDN FEGR

Name	(PLEASE PRINT)	

Address		Apt. #

City	State/Prov.	Zip/Postal Code

Signature (if under 18, a parent or guardian must sign)

Mail to the **Reader Service:**
IN U.S.A.: P.O. Box 1867, Buffalo, NY 14240-1867
IN CANADA: P.O. Box 609, Fort Erie, Ontario L2A 5X3

Not valid for current subscribers to Love Inspired books.

**Are you a subscriber to Love Inspired books
and want to receive the larger-print edition?
Call 1-800-873-8635 or visit www.ReaderService.com.**

* Terms and prices subject to change without notice. Prices do not include applicable taxes. Sales tax applicable in N.Y. Canadian residents will be charged applicable taxes. Offer not valid in Quebec. This offer is limited to one order per household. All orders subject to credit approval. Credit or debit balances in a customer's account(s) may be offset by any other outstanding balance owed by or to the customer. Please allow 4 to 6 weeks for delivery. Offer available while quantities last.

Your Privacy—The Reader Service is committed to protecting your privacy. Our Privacy Policy is available online at www.ReaderService.com or upon request from the Reader Service.

We make a portion of our mailing list available to reputable third parties that offer products we believe may interest you. If you prefer that we not exchange your name with third parties, or if you wish to clarify or modify your communication preferences, please visit us at www.ReaderService.com/consumerschoice or write to us at Reader Service Preference Service, P.O. Box 9062, Buffalo, NY 14269. Include your complete name and address.

LIREG11B

Fairy tales do come true with fan-favorite author

JILLIAN HART

Honor Crosby never thought she would find a man she
could trust again, especially not in an online book group.
But when Honor finds herself heading to Luke McKaslin's
Montana ranch to see if their chemistry works offline,
her fantasy becomes too real. Can Honor believe in love…
even as she falls for Luke?

Montana Cowboy

THE McKASLIN CLAN